Ernest Miller Hemingway was born in 1899. His father was a doctor and he was the second of six children. Their home was at Oak Park, a Chicago suburb.

In 1917 Hemingway joined the Kansas City *Star* as a cub reporter. The following year he volunteered to work as an ambulance driver on the Italian front where he was badly wounded but twice decorated for his services. He returned to America in 1919 and married in 1921. In 1922 he reported on the Greco-Turkish war then two years later resigned from journalism to devote himself to fiction. He settled in Paris where he renewed his earlier friendship with such fellow-American expatriates as Ezra Pound and Gertrude Stein. Their encouragement and criticism were to play a valuable part in the formation of his style.

Hemingway's first two published works were *Three Stories and Ten Poems* and *In Our Time* but it was the satirical novel, *The Torrents of Spring*, which established his name more widely. His international reputation was firmly secured by his next three books: *Fiesta, Men Without Women* and *A Farewell to Arms*. He was passionately involved with bullfighting, big-game hunting and deep-sea fishing, and his writing reflected this. He visited Spain during the Civil War and described his experiences in the bestseller, *For Whom the Bell Tolls*. His direct and deceptively simple style of writing spawned generations of imitators but no equals. Recognition of his position in contemporary literature came in 1954 when he was awarded the Nobel Prize, following the publication of *The Old Man and the Sea*. Ernest Hemingway died in 1961.

By the same author

Stories
Men Without Women
The Snows of Kilimanjaro

Novels
The Torrents of Spring
Fiesta
A Farewell to Arms
To Have and Have Not
For Whom the Bell Tolls
Across the River and Into the Trees
The Old Man and the Sea
Islands in the Stream

General
Death in the Afternoon
Green Hills of Africa
A Moveable Feast

Drama
The Fifth Column

Collected Works
The Essential Hemingway
The First Forty-Nine Stories

ERNEST HEMINGWAY

Winner Take Nothing

A TRIAD PANTHER BOOK
Granada Publishing

Panther Books
Granada Publishing Ltd
8 Grafton Street, London W1X 3LA

Published by Panther Books 1977
Reprinted 1981, 1984, 1985

First published in Great Britain
in *The Fifth Column* and *The First Forty-Nine*
(reissued in 1944 as *The First Forty-Nine Stories*)
by Jonathan Cape Ltd 1939
This selection first published by
Penguin Books Ltd under the
title of *The Short Happy Life of
Francis Macomber* (1963)
Copyright © the Estate of Ernest Hemingway 1939

ISBN 0-586-04462-0

Printed and bound in Great Britain by
Collins, Glasgow

Set in Monotype Garamond

Contents

The Short Happy Life of
Francis Macomber

It was now lunch time and they were all sitting under the double green fly of the dining tent pretending that nothing had happened.

'Will you have lime juice or lemon squash?' Macomber asked.

'I'll have a gimlet,' Robert Wilson told him.

'I'll have a gimlet too. I need something,' Macomber's wife said.

'I suppose it's the thing to do,' Macomber agreed. 'Tell him to make three gimlets.'

The mess boy had started them already, lifting the bottles out of the canvas cooling bags that sweated wet in the wind that blew through the trees that shaded the tents.

'What had I ought to give them?' Macomber asked.

'A quid would be plenty,' Wilson told him. 'You don't want to spoil them.'

'Will the headman distribute it?'

'Absolutely.'

Francis Macomber had, half an hour before, been carried to his tent from the edge of the camp in triumph on the arms and shoulders of the cook, the personal boys, the skinner and the porters. The gun-bearers had taken no part in the demonstration. When the native boys put him down at the door of his tent, he had shaken all their hands, received their congratulations, and then gone into the tent and sat on the bed until his wife came in. She did not speak to him when she came in and he left the tent at once to wash his face and hands in the portable wash basin outside and go over to the dining tent to sit in a comfortable canvas chair in the breeze and the shade.

Mrs Macomber looked at Wilson quickly. She was an extremely handsome and well-kept woman of the beauty and social position which had, five years before, commanded five thousand dollars as the price of endorsing, with photographs, a beauty product which she had never used. She had been married to Francis Macomber for eleven years.

'He is a good lion, isn't he?' Macomber said. His wife looked at him now. She looked at both these men as though she had never seen them before.

One, Wilson, the white hunter, she knew she had never truly seen before. He was about middle height with sandy hair, a stubby moustache, a very red face and extremely cold blue eyes with faint white wrinkles at the corners that grooved merrily when he smiled. He smiled at her now and she looked away from his face at the way his shoulders sloped in the loose tunic he wore with the four big cartridges held in loops where the left breast pocket should have been, at his big brown hands, his old slacks, his very dirty boots, and back to his red face again. She noticed where the baked red of his face stopped in a white line that marked the circle by his Stetson hat that hung now from one of the pegs of the tent pole.

'Well, here's to the lion,' Robert Wilson said. He smiled at her again and, not smiling, she looked curiously at her husband.

Francis Macomber was very tall, very well built if you did not mind that length of bone, dark, his hair cropped like an oarsman, rather thin-lipped, and was considered handsome. He was dressed in the same sort of safari clothes that Wilson wore except that his were new, he was thirty-five years old, kept himself very fit, was good at court games, had a number of big-game fishing records, and had just shown himself, very publicly, to be a coward.

'Here's to the lion,' he said. 'I can't ever thank you for what you did.'

Margaret, his wife, looked away from him and back to Wilson.

'Let's not talk about the lion,' she said.

Wilson looked over at her without smiling and now she smiled at him.

'It's been a very strange day,' she said. 'Hadn't you ought to put your hat on even under the canvas at noon? You told me that, you know.'

'Might put it on,' said Wilson.

'You know you have a very red face, Mr Wilson,' she told him and smiled again.

'Drink,' said Wilson.

'I don't think so,' she said. 'Francis drinks a great deal, but his face is never red.'

'It's red today,' Macomber tried a joke.

'No,' said Margaret. 'It's mine that's red today. But Mr Wilson's is always red.'

'Must be racial,' said Wilson. 'I say, you wouldn't like to drop my beauty as a topic, would you?'

'I've just started on it.'

'Let's chuck it,' said Wilson.

'Conversation is going to be so difficult,' Margaret said.

'Don't be silly, Margot,' her husband said.

'No difficulty,' Wilson said. 'Got a damn fine lion.'

Margot looked at them both and they both saw that she was going to cry. Wilson had seen it coming for a long time and he dreaded it. Macomber was past dreading it.

'I wish it hadn't happened. Oh, I wish it hadn't happened,' she said and started for her tent. She made no noise of crying but they could see that her shoulders were shaking under the rose-coloured, sun-proofed shirt she wore.

'Women upset,' said Wilson to the tall man. 'Amounts to nothing. Strain on the nerves and one thing 'n another.'

'No,' said Macomber. 'I suppose that I rate that for the rest of my life now.'

'Nonsense. Let's have a spot of the giant killer,' said Wilson. 'Forget the whole thing. Nothing to it anyway.'

'We might try,' said Macomber. 'I won't forget what you did for me though.'

'Nothing,' said Wilson. 'All nonsense.'

So they sat there in the shade where the camp was pitched under some wide-topped acacia trees with a boulder-strewn cliff behind them, and a stretch of grass that ran to the bank of a boulder-filled stream in front with forest beyond it, and drank their just-cool lime drinks and avoided one another's eyes while the boys set the table for lunch. Wilson could tell

9

that the boys all knew about it now and when he saw Macomber's personal boy looking curiously at his master while he was putting dishes on the table he snapped at him in Swahili. The boy turned away with his face blank.

'What were you telling him?' Macomber asked.

'Nothing. Told him to look alive or I'd see he got about fifteen of the best.'

'What's that? Lashes?'

'It's quite legal,' Wilson said. 'You're supposed to fine them.'

'Do you still have them whipped?'

'Oh, yes. They could raise a row if they chose to complain. But they don't. They prefer it to the fines.'

'How strange!' said Macomber.

'Not strange, really,' Wilson said. 'Which would you rather do? Take a good birching or lose your pay?'

Then he felt embarrassed at asking it and before Macomber could answer he went on, 'We all take a beating every day, you know, one way or another.'

This was no better. 'Good God,' he thought. 'I am a diplomat, aren't I?'

'Yes, we take a beating,' said Macomber, still not looking at him. 'I'm awfully sorry about that lion business. It doesn't have to go any further, does it? I mean no one will hear about it, will they?'

'You mean will I tell it at the Mathaiga Club?' Wilson looked at him now coldly. He had not expected this. So he's a bloody four-letter man as well as a bloody coward, he thought. I rather liked him too until today. But how is one to know about an American?

'No,' said Wilson. 'I'm a professional hunter. We never talk about our clients. You can be quite easy on that. It's supposed to be bad form to ask us not to talk though.'

He had decided now that to break would be much easier. He would eat, then, by himself and could read a book with his meals. They would eat by themselves. He would see them through the safari on a very formal basis – what was it the French called it? Distinguished consideration – and it would be a damn sight easier than having to go through this emotional trash. He'd insult him and make a good clean break. Then he could read a book with his meals and he'd still be drinking their whisky. That was the phrase for it when a safari went bad. You ran into another white hunter and you asked, 'How is everything going?' and he answered, 'Oh, I'm still drinking their whisky,' and you knew everything had gone to pot.

'I'm sorry,' Macomber said and looked at him with his American face that would stay adolescent until it became middle-aged, and Wilson noted his crew-cropped hair, fine eyes only faintly shifty, good nose, thin lips and handsome jaw. 'I'm sorry I didn't realize that. There are lots of things I don't know.'

So what could he do, Wilson thought. He was all ready to break it off quickly and neatly and here the beggar was apologizing after he had just insulted him. He made one more attempt. 'Don't worry about me talking,' he said. 'I have a living to make. You know in Africa no woman ever misses her lion and no white man ever bolts.'

'I bolted like a rabbit,' Macomber said.

Now what in hell were you going to do about a man who talked like that, Wilson wondered.

Wilson looked at Macomber with his flat, blue, machine-gunner's eyes and the other smiled back at him. He had a pleasant smile if you did not notice how his eyes showed when he was hurt.

'Maybe I can fix it up on buffalo,' he said. 'We're after them next, aren't we?'

'In the morning if you like,' Wilson told him. Perhaps he had been wrong. This was certainly the way to take it. You most certainly could not tell a damned thing about an American. He was all for Macomber again. If you could forget the morning. But, of course, you couldn't. The morning had been about as bad as they come.

'Here comes the Memsahib,' he said. She was walking over from her tent looking refreshed and cheerful and quite lovely. She had a perfect oval face, so perfect that you expected her to be stupid. But she wasn't stupid, Wilson thought, no, not stupid.

'How is the beautiful red-faced Mr Wilson? Are you feeling better, Francis, my pearl?'

'Oh, much,' said Macomber.

'I've dropped the whole thing,' she said, sitting down at the table. 'What importance is there to whether Francis is any good at killing lions? That's not his trade. That's Mr Wilson's trade. Mr Wilson is really very impressive killing anything. You do kill anything, don't you?'

'Oh, anything,' said Wilson. 'Simply anything.' They are, he thought, the hardest in the world; the hardest, the cruellest, the most predatory and the most attractive and their men have softened or gone to pieces nervously as they have hardened. Or is it that they pick men they can handle? They can't know that much at the age they marry, he thought. He was grateful that he had gone through his education on American women before now because this was a very attractive one.

'We're going after buff in the morning,' he told her.

'I'm coming,' she said.

'No you're not.'

'Oh, yes, I am. Mayn't I, Francis?'

'Why not stay in camp?'

'Not for anything,' she said. 'I wouldn't miss something like today for anything.'

When she left, Wilson was thinking, when she went off to cry she seemed a hell of a fine woman. She seemed to understand, to realize, to be hurt for him and for herself and to know how things really stood. She is away for twenty minutes and now she is back, simply enamelled in that American female cruelty. They are the damnedest women. Really the damnedest.

'We'll put on another show for you tomorrow,' Francis Macomber said.

'You're not coming,' Wilson said.

'You're very mistaken,' she told him. 'And I want *so* to see you perform again. You were lovely this morning. That is if blowing things' heads off is lovely.'

'Here's the lunch,' said Wilson. 'You're very merry, aren't you?'

'Why not? I didn't come out here to be dull.'

'Well, it hasn't been dull,' Wilson said. He could see the boulders in the river and the high bank beyond with the trees and he remembered the morning.

'Oh, no,' she said. 'It's been charming. And tomorrow. You don't know how I look forward to tomorrow.'

'That's eland he's offering you,' Wilson said.

'They're the big cowy things that jump like hares, aren't they?'

'I suppose that describes them,' Wilson said.

'It's very good meat,' Macomber said.

'Did you shoot it, Francis?' she asked.

'Yes.'

'They're not dangerous, are they?'

'Only if they fall on you,' Wilson told her.

'I'm so glad.'

'Why not let up on the bitchery just a little, Margot,' Macomber said, cutting the eland steak and putting some mashed potato, gravy and carrot on the down-turned fork that tined through the piece of meat.

'I suppose I could,' she said, 'since you put it so prettily.'

'Tonight we'll have champagne for the lion,' Wilson said. 'It's a bit too hot at noon.'

'Oh, the lion,' Margot said. 'I'd forgotten the lion!'

So, Robert Wilson thought to himself, she *is* giving him a ride, isn't she? Or do you suppose that's her idea of putting up a good show? How should a woman act when she discovers her husband is a bloody coward? She's damn cruel, but they're all cruel. They govern, of course, and to govern one has to be cruel sometimes. Still, I've seen enough of their damn terrorism.

'Have some more eland,' he said to her politely.

That afternoon, late, Wilson and Macomber went out in the motor car with the native driver and the two gun-bearers. Mrs Macomber stayed in the camp. It was too hot to go out, she said, and she was going with them in the early morning.

As they drove off Wilson saw her standing under the big tree looking pretty rather than beautiful in her faintly rosy khaki, her dark brown hair drawn back off her forehead and gathered in a knot low on her neck, her face as fresh, he thought, as though she were in England. She waved to them as the car went off through the swale of high grass and curved around through the trees into the small hills of orchard bush.

In the orchard bush they found a herd of impala, and leaving the car they stalked one old ram with long, widespread horns and Macomber killed it with a very creditable shot that knocked the buck down at a good two hundred yards and sent the herd off bounding wildly and leaping over one another's backs in long, leg-drawn-up leaps as unbelievable and as floating as those one makes sometimes in dreams.

'That was a good shot,' Wilson said. 'They're a small target.'

'Is it a worth-while head?' Macomber asked.

'It's excellent,' Wilson told him. 'You shoot like that and you'll have no trouble.'

'Do you think we'll find buffalo tomorrow?'

'There's a good chance of it. They feed out early in the morning and with luck we may catch them in the open.'

'I'd like to clear away that lion business,' Macomber said. 'It's not very pleasant to have your wife see you do something like that.'

I should think it would be even more unpleasant to do it, Wilson thought, wife or no wife, or to talk about it having done it. But he said, 'I wouldn't think about that any more. Anyone could be upset by his first lion. That's all over.'

But that night after dinner and a whisky and soda by the fire before going to bed, as Francis Macomber lay on his cot with the mosquito bar over him and listened to the night noises it was not all over. It was neither all over nor was it beginning. It was there exactly as it happened with some parts of it indelibly emphasized and he was miserably ashamed of it. But more than shame he felt cold, hollow fear in him. The fear was still there like a cold slimy hollow in all the emptiness where once his confidence had been and it made him feel sick. It was still there with him now.

It had started the night before when he had awakened and heard the lion roaring somewhere up along the river. It was a deep sound and at the end there were sort of coughing grunts that made him seem just outside the tent, and when Francis Macomber woke in the night to hear it he was afraid. He could hear his wife breathing quietly, asleep. There was no one to tell he was afraid, nor to be afraid with him, and, lying alone, he did not know the Somali proverb that says a brave man is always frightened three times by a lion; when he first sees his track, when he first hears him roar and when he first confronts him. Then while they were eating breakfast by lantern light out in the dining tent, before the sun was up, the lion roared again and Francis thought he was just at the edge of camp.

'Sounds like an old-timer,' Robert Wilson said, looking up from his kippers and coffee. 'Listen to him cough.'

'Is he very close?'

'A mile or so up the stream.'

'Will we see him?'

'We'll have a look.'

'Does his roaring carry that far? It sounds as though he were right in camp.'

'Carries a hell of a long way,' said Robert Wilson. 'It's strange the way it carries. Hope he's a shootable cat. The boys said there was a very big one about here.'

'If I get a shot, where should I hit him,' Macomber asked, 'to stop him?'

'In the shoulders,' Wilson said. 'In the neck if you can make it. Shoot for bone. Break him down.'

'I hope I can place it properly,' Macomber said.

'You shoot very well,' Wilson told him. 'Take your time. Make sure of him. The first one in is the one that counts.'

'What range will it be?'

'Can't tell. Lion has something to say about that. Don't shoot unless it's close enough so you can make sure.'

'At under a hundred yards?' Macomber asked.

Wilson looked at him quickly.

'Hundred's about right. Might have to take him a bit under. Shouldn't chance a shot at much over that. A hundred's a decent range. You can hit him wherever you want at that. Here comes the Memsahib.'

'Good morning,' she said. 'Are we going after that lion?'

'As soon as you deal with your breakfast,' Wilson said. 'How are you feeling?'

'Marvellous,' she said. 'I'm very excited.'

'I'll just go and see that everything is ready.' Wilson went off. As he left the lion roared again.

'Noisy beggar,' Wilson said. 'We'll put a stop to that.'

'What's the matter, Francis?' his wife asked him.

'Nothing,' Macomber said.

'Yes, there is,' she said. 'What are you upset about?'

'Nothing,' he said.

'Tell me,' she looked at him. 'Don't you feel well?'

'It's that damned roaring,' he said. 'It's been going on all night, you know.'

'Why didn't you wake me?' she said. 'I'd love to have heard it.'

'I've got to kill the damned thing,' Macomber said, miserably.

'Well, that's what you're out here for, isn't it?'

'Yes. But I'm nervous. Hearing the thing roar gets on my nerves.'

'Well, then, as Wilson said, kill him and stop his roaring.'

'Yes, darling,' said Francis Macomber. 'It sounds easy, doesn't it?'

'You're not afraid, are you?'

'Of course not. But I'm nervous from hearing him roar all night.'

'You'll kill him marvellously,' she said. 'I know you will. I'm awfully anxious to see it.'

'Finish your breakfast and we'll be starting.'

'It's not light yet,' she said. 'This is a ridiculous hour.'

Just then the lion roared in a deep-chested moaning,

suddenly guttural, ascending vibration that seemed to shake the air and ended in a sigh and a heavy, deep-chested grunt.

'He sounds almost here,' Macomber's wife said.

'My God,' said Macomber. 'I hate that damned noise.'

'It's very impressive.'

'Impressive. It's frightful.'

Robert Wilson came up then carrying his short, ugly, shockingly big-bored ·505 Gibbs and grinning.

'Come on,' he said. 'Your gun-bearer has your Springfield and the big gun. Everything's in the car. Have you solids?'

'Yes.'

'I'm ready,' Mrs Macomber said.

'Must make him stop that racket,' Wilson said. 'You get in front. The Memsahib can sit back here with me.'

They climbed into the motor car and, in the grey first daylight, moved off up the river through the trees. Macomber opened the breech of his rifle and saw he had metal-cased bullets, shut the bolt and put the rifle on safety. He saw his hand was trembling. He felt in his pocket for more cartridges and moved his fingers over the cartridges in the loops of his tunic front. He turned back to where Wilson sat in the rear seat of the doorless, box-bodied motor car beside his wife, them both grinning with excitement, and Wilson leaned forward and whispered.

'See the birds dropping. Means the old boy has left his kill.'

On the far bank of the stream Macomber could see, above the trees, vultures circling and plummeting down.

'Chances are he'll come to drink along here,' Wilson whispered. 'Before he goes to lay up. Keep an eye out.'

They were driving slowly along the high bank of the stream which here cut deeply to its boulder-filled bed, and they wound in and out through big trees as they drove. Macomber was watching the opposite bank when he felt Wilson take hold of his arm. The car stopped.

'There he is,' he heard the whisper. 'Ahead and to the right. Get out and take him. He's a marvellous lion.'

Macomber saw the lion now. He was standing almost broadside, his great head up and turned toward them. The early morning breeze that blew toward them was just stirring his dark mane, and the lion looked huge, silhouetted on the rise of bank in the grey morning light, his shoulders heavy, his barrel of a body bulking smoothly.

'How far is he?' asked Macomber, raising his rifle.

'About seventy-five. Get out and take him.'

'Why not shoot from where I am?'

'You don't shoot them from cars,' he heard Wilson saying in his ear. 'Get out. He's not going to stay there all day.'

Macomber stepped out of the curved opening at the side of the front seat, on to the step and down on to the ground. The lion still stood looking majestically and coolly toward this object that his eyes only showed in silhouette, bulking like some super-rhino. There was no man smell carried toward him and he watched the object, moving his great head a little from side to side. Then watching the object, not afraid, but hesitating before going down the bank to drink with such a thing opposite him, he saw a man figure detach itself from it and he turned his heavy head and swung away toward the cover of the trees as he heard a cracking crash and felt the slam of a ·30-06 220-grain solid bullet that bit his flank and ripped in sudden hot scalding nausea through his stomach. He trotted, heavy, big-footed, swinging wounded full-bellied, through the trees toward the tall grass and cover, and the crash came again to go past him ripping the air apart. Then it crashed again and he felt the blow as it hit his lower ribs and ripped on through, blood sudden hot and frothy in his mouth, and he galloped toward the high grass where he could crouch and not be seen and make them bring the crashing thing close enough so he could make a rush and get the man that held it.

Macomber had not thought how the lion felt as he got out of the car. He only knew his hands were shaking and as he walked away from the car it was almost impossible for him to make his legs move. They were stiff in the thighs, but he could feel the muscles fluttering. He raised the rifle, sighted on the junction of the lion's head and shoulders and pulled the trigger. Nothing happened though he pulled until he thought his finger would break. Then he knew he had the safety on and as he lowered the rifle to move the safety over he moved another frozen pace forward, and the lion, seeing his silhouette now clear of the silhouette of the car, turned and started off at a trot, and, as Macomber fired, he heard a whunk that meant the bullet was home; but the lion kept on going. Macomber shot again and everyone saw the bullet throw a spout of dirt beyond the trotting lion. He shot again, remembering to lower his aim, and they all heard the bullet hit, and the lion went into a gallop and was in the tall grass before he had the bolt pushed forward.

Macomber stood there feeling sick at his stomach, his hands that held the Springfield still cocked, shaking, and his wife and Robert Wilson were standing by him. Beside him too were the gun-bearers chattering, in Wakamba.

'I hit him,' Macomber said. 'I hit him twice.'

'You gut-shot him and you hit him somewhere forward,' Wilson said without enthusiasm. The gun-bearers looked very grave. They were silent now.

'You may have killed him,' Wilson went on. 'We'll have to wait a while before we go in to find out.'

'What do you mean?'

'Let him get sick before we follow him up.'

'Oh,' said Macomber.

'He's a hell of a fine lion,' Wilson said cheerfully. 'He's gotten into a bad place though.'

'Why is it bad?'

'Can't see him until you're on him.'

'Oh,' said Macomber.

'Come on,' said Wilson. 'The Memsahib can stay here in the car. We'll go to have a look at the blood spoor.'

'Stay here, Margot,' Macomber said to his wife. His mouth was very dry and it was hard for him to talk.

'Why?' she asked.

'Wilson says to.'

'We're going to have a look,' Wilson said. 'You stay here. You can see even better from here.'

'All right.'

Wilson spoke in Swahili to the driver. He nodded and said, 'Yes, Bwana.'

Then they went down the steep bank and across the stream, climbing over and around the boulders and up the other bank, pulling up by some projecting roots, and along it until they found where the lion had been trotting when Macomber first shot. There was dark blood on the short grass that the gun-bearers pointed out with grass stems, and that ran away behind the river bank trees.

'What do we do?' asked Macomber.

'Not much choice,' said Wilson. 'We can't bring the car over. Bank's too steep. We'll let him stiffen up a bit and then you and I'll go in and have a look for him.'

'Can't we set the grass on fire?' Macomber asked.

'Too green.'

'Can't we send beaters?'

Wilson looked at him appraisingly. 'Of course we can,' he said. 'But it's just a touch murderous. You see we know the lion's wounded. You can drive an unwounded lion – he'll move on ahead of a noise – but a wounded lion's going to charge. You can't see him until you're right on him. He'll make himself perfectly flat in cover you wouldn't think would hide a hare. You can't very well send boys in there to that sort of a show. Somebody bound to get mauled.'

'What about the gun-bearers?'

'Oh, they'll go with us. It's their *shauri*. You see, they signed on for it. They don't look too happy though, do they?'

'I don't want to go in there,' said Macomber. It was out before he knew he'd said it.

'Neither do I,' said Wilson very cheerily. 'Really no choice though.' Then, as an afterthought, he glanced at Macomber and saw suddenly how he was trembling and the pitiful look on his face.

'You don't have to go in, of course,' he said. 'That's what I'm hired for, you know. That's why I'm so expensive.'

'You mean you'd go in by yourself? Why not leave him there?'

Robert Wilson, whose entire occupation had been with the lion and the problem he presented, and who had not been thinking about Macomber except to note that he was rather windy, suddenly felt as though he had opened the wrong door in an hotel and seen something shameful.

'What do you mean?'

'Why not just leave him?'

'You mean pretend to ourselves he hasn't been hit?'

'No. Just drop it.'

'It isn't done.'

'Why not?'

'For one thing, he's certain to be suffering. For another, someone else might run on to him.'

'I see.'

'But you don't have to have anything to do with it.'

'I'd like to,' Macomber said. 'I'm just scared, you know.'

'I'll go ahead when we go in,' Wilson said, 'with Kongoni tracking. You keep behind me and a little to one side. Chances are we'll hear him growl. If we see him we'll both shoot. Don't worry about anything. I'll keep you backed up. As a matter of fact, you know, perhaps you'd better not go. It might be much better. Why don't you go over and join the Memsahib while I just get it over with?'

'No, I want to go.'

'All right,' said Wilson. 'But don't go in if you don't want to. This is my *shauri* now, you know.'

'I want to go,' said Macomber.

They sat under a tree and smoked.

'Want to go back and speak to the Memsahib while we're waiting?' Wilson asked.

'No.'

'I'll just step back and tell her to be patient.'

'Good,' said Macomber. He sat there, sweating under arms, his mouth dry, his stomach hollow feeling, wanting to find courage to tell Wilson to go on and finish off the lion without him. He could not know that Wilson was furious because he had not noticed the state he was in earlier and sent him back to his wife. While he sat there Wilson came up. 'I have your big gun,' he said. 'Take it. We've given him time, I think. Come on.'

Macomber took the big gun and Wilson said:

'Keep behind me and about five yards to the right and do exactly as I tell you.' Then he spoke in Swahili to the two gun-bearers who looked the picture of gloom.

'Let's go,' he said.

'Could I have a drink of water?' Macomber asked. Wilson spoke to the older gun-bearer, who wore a canteen on his belt and the man unbuckled it, unscrewed the top and handed it to Macomber, who took it noticing how heavy it seemed and how hairy and shoddy the felt covering was in his hand. He raised it to drink and looked ahead at the high grass with the flat-topped trees behind it. A breeze was blowing toward them and the grass rippled gently in the wind. He looked at the gun-bearer and he could see the gun-bearer was suffering too with fear.

Thirty-five yards into the grass the big lion lay flattened out along the ground. His ears were back and his only movement was a slight twitching up and down of his long, black-tufted tail. He had turned at bay as soon as he had reached this cover and he was sick with the wound through his full belly, and weakening with the wound through his lungs that brought a thin foamy red to his mouth each time he breathed. His flanks were wet and hot and flies were on the little opening the solid bullets had made in his tawny hide, and his big yellow eyes, narrowed with hate, looked straight ahead, only blinking when the pain came as he breathed, and his claws dug in the soft baked earth. All of him, pain, sickness, hatred and all of his remaining strength, was tightening into an absolute concentration for a rush. He could hear the men talking and he waited, gathering all of himself into this preparation for a charge as soon as the men would come into the grass. As he heard their voices his tail stiffened to twitch up and down, and, as they came into the edge of the grass, he made a coughing grunt and charged.

Kongoni, the old gun-bearer, in the lead watching the blood

spoor, Wilson watching the grass for any movement, his big gun ready, the second gun-bearer looking ahead and listening, Macomber close to Wilson, his rifle cocked, they had just moved into the grass when Macomber heard the blood-choked coughing grunt, and saw the swishing rush in the grass. The next thing he knew he was running, running wildly, in panic in the open, running toward the stream.

He heard the *ca-ra-wong!* of Wilson's big rifle, and again in a second crashing *carawong!* and turning saw the lion, horrible-looking now, with half his head seeming to be gone, crawling toward Wilson in the edge of the tall grass while the red-faced man worked the bolt on the short ugly rifle and aimed carefully as another blasting *carawong!* came from the muzzle, and the crawling, heavy, yellow bulk of the lion stiffened and the huge, mutilated head slid forward and Macomber, standing by himself in the clearing where he had run, holding a loaded rifle, while two black men and a white man looked back at him in contempt, knew the lion was dead. He came toward Wilson, his tallness all seeming a naked reproach, and Wilson looked at him and said:

'Want to take pictures?'

'No,' he said.

That was all anyone had said until they reached the motor car. Then Wilson had said:

'Hell of a fine lion. Boys will skin him out. We might as well stay here in the shade.'

Macomber's wife had not looked at him nor he at her and he had sat by her in the back seat with Wilson sitting in the front seat. Once he had reached over and taken his wife's hand without looking at her and she had removed her hand from his. Looking across the stream to where the gun-bearers were skinning out the lion he could see that she had been able to see the whole thing. While they sat there his wife had reached forward and put her hand on Wilson's shoulder. He turned and she had leaned forward over the low seat and kissed him on the mouth.

'Oh, I say,' said Wilson, going redder than his natural baked colour.

'Mr Robert Wilson,' she said. 'The beautifully red-faced Mr Robert Wilson.'

Then she sat down beside Macomber again and looked away across the stream to where the lion lay, with uplifted, white-muscled tendon-marked naked forearms, and white bloating belly, as the black men fleshed away the skin. Finally the gun-bearers brought the skin over, wet and heavy, and climbed in behind with it, rolling it up before they got in, and the motor car started. No one had said anything more until they were back in camp.

That was the story of the lion. Macomber did not know how the lion had felt before he started his rush, nor during it when the unbelievable smash of the ·505 with a muzzle velocity of two tons had hit him in the mouth, nor what kept him coming after that, when the second ripping crash had smashed his hind quarters and he had come crawling on toward the crashing, blasting thing that had destroyed him. Wilson knew something about it and only expressed it by saying, 'Damned fine lion', but Macomber did not know how Wilson felt about things either. He did not know how his wife felt except that she was through with him.

His wife had been through with him before but it never lasted. He was very wealthy, and would be much wealthier, and he knew she would not leave him ever now. That was one of the few things he really knew. He knew about that, about motor cycles - that was earliest - about motor cars, about duck-shooting, about fishing, trout, salmon and big-sea, about sex in books, many books, too many books, about all court games, about dogs, not much about horses, about hanging on to his money, about most of the other things his world dealt in, and about his wife not leaving him. His wife had been a great beauty and she was still a great beauty in Africa, but she was not a great enough beauty any more at home to be able to leave him and better herself and she knew it and he knew it. She had missed the chance to leave him and he knew it. If he had been better with women she would probably have started to worry about him getting another new, beautiful wife; but she knew too much about him to worry about him either. Also, he had always had a great tolerance which seemed the nicest thing about him if it were not the most sinister.

All in all they were known as a comparatively happily married couple, one of those whose disruption is often rumoured but never occurs, and as the society columnist put it, they were adding more than a spice of *adventure* to their much envied and ever-enduring *Romance* by a *Safari* in what was known as *Darkest Africa* until the Martin Johnsons lighted it on so many silver screens where they were pursuing *Old Simba* the lion, the buffalo, *Tembo* the elephant and as well collecting specimens for the Museum of Natural History. This same columnist had reported them *on the verge* at least three times in the past and they had been. But they always made it up. They had a sound basis of union. Margot was too beautiful for Macomber to divorce her and Macomber had too much money for Margot ever to leave him.

It was now about three o'clock in the morning and Francis Macomber, who had been asleep a little while after he had stopped thinking about the lion, wakened and then slept again, woke suddenly, frightened in a dream of the bloody-headed lion, standing over him, and listening while his heart pounded, he realized that his wife was not in the other cot in the tent. He lay awake with that knowledge for two hours.

At the end of that time his wife came into the tent, lifted her mosquito bar and crawled cosily into bed.

'Where have you been?' Macomber asked in the darkness.

'Hello,' she said. 'Are you awake?'

'Where have you been?'

'I just went out to get a breath of air.'

'You did, like hell.'

'What do you want me to say, darling?'

'Where have you been?'

'Out to get a breath of air.'

'That's a new name for it. You *are* a bitch.'

'Well, you're a coward.'

'All right,' he said. 'What of it?'

'Nothing so far as I'm concerned. But please let's not talk, darling, because I'm very sleepy.'

'You think that I'll take anything.'

'I know you will, sweet.'

'Well, I won't.'

'Please, darling, let's not talk. I'm so very sleepy.'

'There wasn't going to be any of that. You promised there wouldn't be.'

'Well, there is now,' she said sweetly.

'You said if we made this trip that there would be none of that. You promised.'

'Yes, darling. That's the way I meant it to be. But the trip was spoiled yesterday. We don't have to talk about it, do we?'

'You don't wait long when you have an advantage, do you?'

'Please, let's not talk. I'm so sleepy, darling.'

'I'm going to talk.'

'Don't mind me then, because I'm going to sleep.' And she did.

At breakfast they were all three at the table before daylight and Francis Macomber found that, of all the many men that he had hated, he hated Robert Wilson the most.

'Sleep well?' Wilson asked in his throaty voice, filling a pipe.

'Did you?'

'Topping,' the white hunter told him.

You bastard, thought Macomber, you insolent bastard.

So she woke him when she came in, Wilson thought, looking at them both with his flat, cold eyes. Well, why doesn't he keep his wife where she belongs? What does he think I am, a bloody plaster saint? Let him keep her where she belongs. It's his own fault.

'Do you think we'll find buffalo?' Margot asked, pushing away a dish of apricots.

'Chance of it,' Wilson said and smiled at her. 'Why don't you stay in camp?'

'Not for anything,' she told him.

'Why not order her to stay in camp?' Wilson said to Macomber.

'You order her,' said Macomber coldly.

'Let's not have any ordering, nor,' turning to Macomber, 'any silliness, Francis,' Margot said quite pleasantly.

'Are you ready to start?' Macomber asked.

'Any time,' Wilson told him. 'Do you want the Memsahib to go?'

'Does it make any difference whether I do or not?'

The hell with it, thought Robert Wilson. The utter complete hell with it. So this is what it's going to be like. Well, this is what it's going to be like, then.

'Makes no difference,' he said.

'You're sure you wouldn't like to stay in camp with her yourself and let me go out and hunt the buffalo?' Macomber asked.

'Can't do that,' said Wilson. 'Wouldn't talk rot if I were you.'

'I'm not talking rot. I'm disgusted.'

'Bad word, disgusted.'

'Francis, will you please try to speak sensibly?' his wife said.

'I speak too damned sensibly,' Macomber said. 'Did you ever eat such filthy food?'

'Something wrong with the food?' asked Wilson quietly.

'No more than with everything else.'

'I'd pull yourself together, laddybuck,' Wilson said very quietly. 'There's a boy waits at table that understands a little English.'

'The hell with him.'

Wilson stood up and puffing on his pipe strolled away, speaking a few words in Swahili to one of the gun-bearers who was standing waiting for him. Macomber and his wife sat on at the table. He was staring at his coffee cup.

'If you make a scene I'll leave you, darling,' Margot said quietly.

'No, you won't.'

'You can try and see.'

'You won't leave me.'

'No,' she said. 'I won't leave you and you'll behave yourself.'

'Behave myself? That's a way to talk. Behave myself.'

'Yes. Behave yourself.'

'Why don't *you* try behaving?'

'I've tried it so long. So very long.'

'I hate that red-faced swine,' Macomber said. 'I loathe the sight of him.'

'He's really *very* nice.'

'Oh, *shut up*,' Macomber almost shouted. Just then the car came up and stopped in front of the dining tent and the driver and the two gun-bearers got out. Wilson walked over and looked at the husband and wife sitting there at the table.

'Going shooting?' he asked.

'Yes,' said Macomber, standing up. 'Yes.'

'Better bring a woolly. It will be cool in the car,' Wilson said.

'I'll get my leather jacket,' Margot said.

'The boy has it,' Wilson told her. He climbed into the front with the driver and Francis Macomber and his wife sat, not speaking, in the back seat.

Hope the silly beggar doesn't take a notion to blow the back of my head off, Wilson thought to himself. Women *are* a nuisance on safari.

The car was grinding down to cross the river at a pebbly ford in the grey daylight and then climbed, angling up the steep bank, where Wilson had ordered a way shovelled out the day before so they could reach the parklike wooded rolling country on the far side.

It was a good morning, Wilson thought. There was a heavy dew and as the wheels went through the grass and low bushes he could smell the odour of the crushed fronds. It was an odour like verbena and he liked this early morning smell of the dew, the crushed bracken and the look of the tree trunks showing black through the early morning mist, as the car made its way through the untracked, parklike country. He had put the two in the back seat out of his mind now and was thinking about buffalo. The buffalo that he was after stayed in the daytime in a thick swamp where it was impossible to get a shot, but in the night they fed out into an open stretch of country and if he could come between them and their swamp with the car, Macomber would have a good chance at them in the open. He did not want to hunt buff with Macomber in thick cover. He did not want to hunt buff or anything else with Macomber at all, but he was a professional hunter and he had hunted with some rare ones in his time. If they got buff today there would only be rhino to come and the poor man would have gone through his dangerous game and things might pick up. He'd have nothing more to do with the woman and Macomber would get over that too. He must have gone through plenty of that before by the look of things. Poor beggar. He must have a way of getting over it. Well, it was the poor sod's own bloody fault.

He, Robert Wilson, carried a double size cot on safari to accommodate any windfalls he might receive. He had hunted for a certain clientele, the international, fast, sporting set, where the women did not feel they were getting their money's worth unless they shared that cot with the white hunter. He despised them when he was away from them although he liked some of them well enough at the time, but he made his living by them; and their standards were his standards as long as they were hiring him.

They were his standards in all except the shooting. He had his own standards about the killing and they could live up to them or get someone else to hunt them. He knew too, that they all respected him for this. This Macomber was an odd one though. Damned if he wasn't. Now the wife. Well, the wife. Yes, the wife. Mm, the wife. Well, he'd dropped all that. He looked around at them. Macomber sat grim and furious. Margot smiled at him. She looked younger today, more innocent and fresher and not so professionally beautiful. What's in her heart God knows, Wilson thought. She hadn't talked much last night. At that it was a pleasure to see her.

The motor car climbed up a slight rise and went on through the trees and then out into a grassy prairie-like opening and kept in the shelter of the trees along the edge, the driver going slowly and Wilson looking carefully out across the prairie and all along its far side. He stopped the car and studied the opening with his field glasses. Then he motioned the driver to go on and the car moved slowly along, the driver avoiding wart-hog holes and driving around the mud castles ants had built. Then, looking across the opening, Wilson suddenly turned and said:

'By God, there they are!'

And looking where he pointed, while the car jumped forward and Wilson spoke in rapid Swahili to the driver, Macomber saw three huge, black animals looking almost cylindrical in their long heaviness, like big black tank cars, moving at a gallop across the far edge of the open prairie. They moved at a stiff-necked, stiff-bodied gallop and he could see the upswept wide black horns on their heads as they galloped heads out, the heads not moving.

'They're three old bulls,' Wilson said. 'We'll cut them off before they get to the swamp.'

The car was going a wild forty-five miles an hour across the open, and as Macomber watched, the buffalo got bigger and bigger until he could see the grey, hairless, scabby look of one huge bull and how his neck was a part of his shoulders and the shiny black of his horns as he galloped a little behind the others that were strung out in that steady plunging gait; and then, the car swaying as though it had just jumped a road, they drew up close and he could see the plunging hugeness of the bull, and the dust in his sparsely haired hide, the wide boss of horn and his outstretched, wide-nostrilled muzzle, and he was raising his rifle when Wilson shouted, 'Not from the car, you fool!' and he had no fear, only hatred of Wilson, while the brakes clamped on and the car skidded, ploughing sideways to an almost stop and Wilson was out on one side and he on the other, stumbling as his feet hit the still speeding-by of the earth, and then he was shooting at the bull as he moved away, hearing the bullets whunk into him, emptying his rifle at him as he moved steadily away, finally remembering to get his shots forward into the shoulder, and as he fumbled to re-load, he saw the bull was down. Down on his knees, his big head tossing, and seeing the other two still galloping he shot at the leader and hit him. He shot again and missed and he heard the *carawonging* roar as Wilson shot and saw the leading bull slide forward on to his nose.

'Get that other,' Wilson said. 'Now you're shooting!'

But the other bull was moving steadily at the same gallop and he missed, throwing a spout of dirt, and Wilson missed and the dust rose in a cloud and Wilson shouted, 'Come on. He's too far!' and grabbed his arm and they were in the car again, Macomber and Wilson hanging on to the sides and rocketing swayingly over the uneven ground, drawing up on the steady, plunging, heavy-necked, straight-moving gallop of the bull.

They were behind him and Macomber was filling his rifle, dropping shells on to the ground, jamming it, clearing the jam, then they were almost up with the bull when Wilson yelled 'Stop!' and the car skidded so that it almost swung over and Macomber fell forward on to his feet, slammed his bolt forward and fired as far forward as he could aim into the galloping, rounded black back, aimed and shot again, then again, and the bullets, all of them hitting, had no effect on the buffalo that he could see. Then Wilson shot, the roar deafening him, and he could see the bull stagger. Macomber shot again, aiming carefully, and down he came, on to his knees.

'All right,' Wilson said. 'Nice work. That's the three.'

Macomber felt a drunken elation.

'How many times did you shoot?' he asked.

'Just three,' Wilson said. 'You killed the first bull. The biggest one. I helped you finish the other two. Afraid they might have got into cover. You had them killed. I was just mopping up a little. You shot damn well.'

'Let's go to the car,' said Macomber. 'I want a drink.'

'Got to finish off that buff first,' Wilson told him. The buffalo was on his knees and he jerked his head furiously and bellowed in pig-eyed roaring rage as they came toward him.

'Watch he doesn't get up,' Wilson said. Then, 'Get a little broadside and take him in the neck just behind the ear.'

Macomber aimed carefully at the centre of the huge, jerking, rage-driven neck and shot. At the shot the head dropped forward.

'That does it,' said Wilson. 'Got the spine. They're a hell of a looking thing, aren't they?'

'Let's get the drink,' said Macomber. In his life he had never felt so good.

In the car Macomber's wife sat very white faced. 'You were marvellous, darling,' she said to Macomber. 'What a ride.'

'Was it rough?' Wilson asked.

'It was frightful. I've never been more frightened in my life.'

'Let's all have a drink,' Macomber said.

'By all means,' said Wilson. 'Give it to the Memsahib.' She drank the neat whisky from the flask and shuddered a little when she swallowed. She handed the flask to Macomber who handed it to Wilson.

'It was frightfully exciting,' she said. 'It's given me a dreadful headache. I didn't know you were allowed to shoot them from cars though.'

'No one shot from cars,' said Wilson coldly.

'I mean chase them from cars.'

'Wouldn't ordinarily,' Wilson said. 'Seemed sporting enough to me though while we were doing it. Taking more chance driving that way across the plain full of holes and one thing and another than hunting on foot. Buffalo could have charged us each time we shot if he liked. Gave him every chance. Wouldn't mention it to anyone though. It's illegal if that's what you mean.'

'It seemed very unfair to me,' Margo said, 'chasing those big helpless things in a motor car.'

'Did it?' said Wilson.

'What would happen if they heard about it in Nairobi?'

'I'd lose my licence for one thing. Other unpleasantnesses,' Wilson said, taking a drink from the flask. 'I'd be out of business.'

'Really?'

'Yes, really.'

'Well,' said Macomber, and he smiled for the first time all day. 'Now she has something on you.'

'You have such a pretty way of putting things, Francis,'

Margot Macomber said. Wilson looked at them both. If a four-letter man marries a five-letter woman, he was thinking, what number of letters would their children be? What he said was 'We lost a gun-bearer. Did you notice it?'

'My God, no,' Macomber said.

'Here he comes,' Wilson said. 'He's all right. He must have fallen off when we left the first bull.'

Approaching them, was the middle-aged gun-bearer, limping along in his knitted cap, khaki tunic, shorts and rubber sandals, gloomy-faced and disgusted looking. As he came up he called out to Wilson in Swahili and they all saw the change in the white hunter's face.

'What does he say?' asked Margot.

'He says the first bull got up and went into the bush,' Wilson said with no expression in his voice.

'Oh,' said Macomber blankly.

'Then it's going to be just like the lion,' said Margot, full of anticipation.

'It's not going to be a damned bit like the lion,' Wilson told her. 'Did you want another drink, Macomber?'

'Thanks, yes,' Macomber said. He expected the feeling he had had about the lion to come back but it did not. For the first time in his life he really felt wholly without fear. Instead of fear he had a feeling of definite elation.

'We'll go and have a look at the second bull,' Wilson said. 'I'll tell the driver to put the car in the shade.'

'What are you going to do?' asked Margot Macomber.

'Take a look at the buff,' Wilson said.

'I'll come.'

'Come along.'

The three of them walked over to where the second buffalo bulked blackly in the open, head forward on the grass, the massive horns swung wide.

'He's a very good head,' Wilson said. 'That's close to a fifty-inch spread.'

Macomber was looking at him with delight.

'He's hateful looking,' said Margot. 'Can't we go into the shade?'

'Of course,' Wilson said. 'Look,' he said to Macomber, and pointed. 'See that patch of bush?'

'Yes.'

'That's where the first bull went in. The gun-bearer said when he fell off the bull was down. He was watching us helling along and the other two buff galloping. When he looked up there was the bull up and looking at him. Gun-bearer ran like hell and the bull went off slowly into that bush.'

'Can we go in after him now?' asked Macomber eagerly.

Wilson looked at him appraisingly. Damned if this isn't a strange one, he thought. Yesterday he's scared sick and today he's a ruddy fire-eater.

'No, we'll give him a while.'

'Let's please go into the shade,' Margot said. Her face was white and she looked ill.

They made their way to the car where it stood under a single wide-spreading tree and all climbed in.

'Chances are he's dead in there,' Wilson remarked. 'After a little we'll have a look.'

Macomber felt a wild unreasonable happiness that he had never known before.

'By God, that was a chase,' he said. 'I've never felt any such feeling. Wasn't it marvellous, Margot?'

'I hated it.'

'Why?'

'I hated it,' she said bitterly. 'I loathed it.'

'You know, I don't think I'd ever be afraid of anything again,' Macomber said to Wilson. 'Something happened in me after we first saw the buff and started after him. Like a dam bursting. It was pure excitement.'

'Cleans out your liver,' said Wilson. 'Damn funny things happen to people.'

Macomber's face was shining. 'You know, something did happen to me,' he said, 'I feel absolutely different.'

His wife said nothing and eyed him strangely. She was sitting far back in the seat and Macomber was sitting forward talking to Wilson who turned sideways talking over the back of the front seat.

'You know, I'd like to try another lion,' Macomber said. 'I'm not really afraid of them now. After all, what can they do to you?'

'That's it,' said Wilson. 'Worst one can do is kill you. How does it go? Shakespeare. Damned good. See if I can remember. Oh, damned good. Used to quote it to myself at one time. Let's see. "By my troth, I care not; a man can die but once; we owe God a death, and let it go which way it will he that dies this year is quit for the next." Damned fine, eh?'

He was very embarrassed, having brought out this thing he had lived by, but he had seen men come of age before and it always moved him. It was not a matter of their twenty-first birthday.

It had taken a strange chance of hunting, a sudden precipitation into action without opportunity for worrying beforehand, to bring this about with Macomber, but regardless of how it had happened it had most certainly happened. Look at the beggar now, Wilson thought. Sometimes all their lives. Their figures stay boyish when they're fifty. The great American boy-men. Damned strange people. But he liked this Macomber now. Damned strange fellow. Probably meant the end of cuckoldry too. Well, that would be a damned good thing. Damned good thing. Beggar had probably been afraid all his life. Don't know what started it. But over now. Hadn't had time to be afraid with the buff. That and being angry too. Motor car too. Motor cars made it familiar. Be a damn fire-eater now. He'd seen it in the war work the same way. More of a change than any loss of virginity. Fear gone like an operation. Something else grew in its place. Main thing a man had. Made him into a man. Women knew it too. No bloody fear.

From the far corner of the seat Margot Macomber looked at the two of them. There was no change in Wilson. She saw Wilson as she had seen him the day before when she had first realized what his great talent was. But she saw the change in Francis Macomber now.

'Do you have that feeling of happiness about what's going to happen?' Macomber asked, still exploring his new wealth.

'You're not supposed to mention it,' Wilson said, looking

in the other's face. 'Much more fashionable to say you're scared. Mind you, you'll be scared too, plenty of times.'

'But you *have* a feeling of happiness about action to come?'

'Yes,' said Wilson. 'There's that. Doesn't do to talk too much about all this. Talk the whole thing away. No pleasure in anything if you mouth it up too much.'

'You're both talking rot,' said Margot. 'Just because you've chased some helpless animals in a motor car you talk like heroes.'

'Sorry,' said Wilson. 'I have been gassing too much.' She's worried about it already, he thought.

'If you don't know what we're talking about, why not keep out of it?' Macomber asked his wife.

'You've gotten awfully brave, awfully suddenly,' his wife said contemptuously, but her contempt was not secure. She was very afraid of something.

Macomber laughed, a very natural laugh. 'You know I *have*,' he said. 'I really have.'

'Isn't it sort of late?' Margot said bitterly. Because she had done the best she could for many years back and the way they were together now was no one person's fault.

'Not for me,' said Macomber.

Margot said nothing but sat back in the corner of the seat.

'Do you think we've given him time enough?' Macomber asked Wilson cheerfully.

'We might have a look,' Wilson said. 'Have you any solids left?'

'The gun-bearer has some.'

Wilson called in Swahili and the older gun-bearer, who was skinning out one of the heads, straightened up, pulled a box of solids out of his pocket, and brought them over to Macomber, who filled his magazine and put the remaining shells in his pocket.

'You might as well shoot the Springfield,' Wilson said. 'You're used to it. We'll leave the Mannlicher in the car with the Memsahib. Your gun-bearer can carry your heavy gun. I've this damned cannon. Now let me tell you about them.' He had saved this until the last because he did not want to worry Macomber. 'When a buff comes he comes with his head high and thrust straight out. The boss of the horns covers any sort of brain shot. The only shot is straight into the nose. The only other shot is into his chest, or, if you're to one side, into the neck or the shoulders. After they've been hit once they take a hell of a lot of killing. Don't try anything fancy. Take the easiest shot there is. They've finished skinning out that head now. Should we get started?'

He called to the gun-bearers, who came up wiping their hands, and the older one got into the back.

'I'll only take Kongoni,' Wilson said. 'The other can watch to keep the birds away.'

As the car moved slowly across the open space toward the island of bushy trees that ran in a tongue of foliage along a dry water-course that cut the open swale, Macomber felt his heart pounding and his mouth was dry again, but it was excitement, not fear.

'Here's where he went in,' Wilson said. Then to the gun-bearer in Swahili, 'Take the blood spoor.'

The car was parallel to the patch of brush. Macomber, Wilson and the gun-bearer got down. Macomber, looking back, saw his wife, with the rifle by her side, looking at him. He waved to her and she did not wave back.

The brush was very thick ahead and the ground was dry. The middle-aged gun-bearer was sweating heavily and Wilson had his hat down over his eyes and his red neck showed just ahead of Macomber. Suddenly the gun-bearer said something in Swahili to Wilson and ran forward.

'He's dead in there,' Wilson said. 'Good work,' and he turned to grip Macomber's hand and as they shook hands, grinning at each other, the gun-bearer shouted wildly and they saw him coming out of the bush sideways, fast as a crab, and the bull coming, nose out, mouth tight closed, blood dripping, massive head straight out, coming in a charge, his little pig eyes bloodshot as he looked at them. Wilson, who was ahead, was kneeling shooting, and Macomber, as he fired, unhearing his shot in the roaring of Wilson's gun, saw fragments like slate burst from the huge boss of the horns, and the head jerked; he shot again at the wide nostrils and saw the horns jolt again and fragments fly, and he did not see Wilson now and, aiming carefully, shot again with the buffalo's huge bulk almost on him and his rifle almost level with the coming head, nose out, and he could see the little wicked eyes and the head started to lower, and he felt a sudden white-hot, blinding flash explode inside his head and that was all he ever felt.

Wilson had ducked to one side to get in a shoulder shot. Macomber had stood solid and shot for the nose, shooting a touch high each time and hitting the heavy horns, splintering and chipping them like hitting a slate roof, and Mrs Macomber in the car, had shot at the buffalo with the 6·5 Mannlicher as it seemed about to gore Macomber and had hit her husband about two inches up and a little to one side of the base of his skull.

Francis Macomber lay now, face down, not two yards from where the buffalo lay on his side and his wife knelt over him with Wilson beside her.

'I wouldn't turn him over,' Wilson said.

The woman was crying hysterically.

'I'd get back in the car,' Wilson said. 'Where's the rifle?'

She shook her head, her face contorted. The gun-bearer picked up the rifle.

'Leave it as it is,' said Wilson. Then, 'Go get Abdulla so that he may witness the manner of the accident.'

He knelt down, took a handkerchief from his pocket, and spread it over Francis Macomber's crew-cropped head where it lay. The blood sank into the dry, loose earth.

Wilson stood up and saw the buffalo on his side, his legs out, his thinly-haired belly crawling with ticks. 'Hell of a good bull,' his brain registered automatically. 'A good fifty inches, or better. Better.' He called to the driver and told him to spread a blanket over the body and stay by it. Then he walked over to the motor car where the woman sat crying in the corner.

'That was a pretty thing to do,' he said in a toneless voice. 'He *would* have left you too.'

'Stop it,' she said.

'Of course it's an accident,' he said. 'I know that.'

'Stop it,' she said.

'Don't worry,' he said. 'There will be a certain amount of unpleasantness but I will have some photographs taken that will be very useful at the inquest. There's the testimony of the gun-bearers and the driver too. You're perfectly all right.'

'Stop it,' she said.

'There's a hell of a lot to be done,' he said. 'And I'll have to send a truck off to the lake to wireless for a plane to take the three of us into Nairobi. Why didn't you poison him? That's what they do in England.'

'Stop it. Stop it. Stop it,' the woman cried.

Wilson looked at her with his flat blue eyes.

'I'm through now,' he said. 'I was a little angry. I'd begun to like your husband.'

'Oh, please stop it,' she said. 'Please, please stop it.'

'That's better,' Wilson said. 'Please is much better. Now I'll stop.'

The Capital of the World

Madrid is full of boys named Paco, which is the diminutive of the name Francisco, and there is a Madrid joke about a father who came to Madrid and inserted an advertisement in the personal columns of *El Liberal* which said: PACO MEET ME AT HOTEL MONTANA NOON TUESDAY ALL IS FORGIVEN PAPA, and how a squadron of Guardia Civil had to be called out to disperse the eight hundred young men who answered the advertisement. But this Paco, who waited on table at the Pension Luarca, had no father to forgive him, nor anything for the father to forgive. He had two older sisters who were chambermaids at the Luarca, who had gotten their place through coming from the same village as a former Luarca chambermaid who had proven hardworking and honest and hence given her village and its products a good name; and these sisters had paid his way on the autobus to Madrid and gotten him his job as an apprentice waiter. He came from a village in a part of Extremadura where conditions were incredibly primitive, food scarce, and comforts unknown, and he had worked hard ever since he could remember.

He was a well-built boy with very black, rather curly hair, good teeth and a skin that his sisters envied, and he had a ready and unpuzzled smile. He was fast on his feet and did his work well and he loved his sisters, who seemed beautiful and unsophisticated; he loved Madrid, which was still an unbelievable place, and he loved his work which, done under bright lights, with clean linen, the wearing of evening clothes, and abundant food in the kitchen, seemed romantically beautiful.

There were from eight to a dozen other people who lived at the Luarca and ate in the dining-room, but for Paco, the youngest of the three waiters who served at table, the only ones who really existed were the bull-fighters.

Second-rate matadors lived at that pension because the address in the Calle San Jeronimo was good, the food was excellent and the room and board was cheap. It is necessary for a bull-fighter to give the appearance, if not of prosperity, at least of respectability, since decorum and dignity rank above courage as the virtues most highly prized in Spain, and bull-fighters stayed at the Luarca until their last pesetas were gone. There is no record of any bull-fighter having left the Luarca for a better or more expensive hotel; second-rate bull-fighters never became first rate; but the descent from the Luarca was swift since anyone could stay there who was making anything at all and a bill was never presented to a guest unasked until the woman who ran the place knew that the case was hopeless.

At this time there were three full matadors living at the Luarca as well as two very good picadors, and one excellent banderillero. The Luarca was luxury for the picadors and the banderilleros who, with their families in Seville, required lodging in Madrid during the spring season; but they were well paid and in the fixed employ of fighters who were heavily contracted during the coming season and the three of these subalterns would probably make much more apiece than any of the three matadors. Of the three matadors one was ill and trying to conceal it; one had passed his short vogue as a novelty; and the third was a coward.

The coward had at one time, until he had received a peculiar atrocious horn wound in the lower abdomen at the start of his first season as a full matador, been exceptionally brave and remarkably skilful and he still had many of the hearty manner-isms of his days of success. He was jovial to excess and laughed constantly with and without provocation. He had, when successful, been very addicted to practical jokes, but he had given them up now. They took an assurance that he did not feel. This matador had an intelligent, very open face and he carried himself with much style.

The matador who was ill was careful never to show it and was meticulous about eating a little of all the dishes that were presented at the table. He had a great many handkerchiefs which he laundered himself in his room and, lately, he had been selling his fighting suits. He had sold one, cheaply, before Christmas and another in the first week of April. They had been very expensive suits, had always been well kept and he had one more. Before he had become ill he had been a very promising, even a sensational, fighter and, while he himself could not read, he had clippings which said that in his debut in Madrid he had been better than Belmonte. He ate alone at a small table and looked up very little.

The matador who had once been a novelty was very short and brown and very dignified. He also ate alone at a separate table and he smiled very rarely and never laughed. He came from Valladolid, where the people are extremely serious, and he was a capable matador; but his style had become old-fashioned before he had ever succeeded in endearing himself to the public through his virtues, which were courage and a calm capability, and his name on a poster would draw no one to a bull ring. His novelty had been that he was so short that he could scarcely see over the bull's withers, but there were other short fighters, and he had never succeeded in imposing himself on the public's fancy.

Of the picadors one was a thin, hawk-faced, grey-haired man, lightly built, but with legs and arms like iron, who always wore cattlemen's boots under his trousers, drank too much every evening and gazed amorously at any woman in the pension. The other was huge, dark, brown-faced, good-looking, with black hair like an Indian and enormous hands. Both were great picadors although the first was reputed to have lost much of his ability through drink and dissipation, and the second was said to be too headstrong and quarrelsome to stay with any matador more than a single season.

The banderillero was middle-aged, grey, cat-quick in spite of his years and, sitting at the table, he looked a moderately prosperous business man. His legs were still good for this season, and when they should go he was intelligent and experienced enough to keep regularly employed for a long time. The difference would be that when his speed of foot would be gone he would always be frightened where now he was assured and calm in the ring and out of it.

On this evening everyone had left the dining-room except the hawk-faced picador who drank too much, the birth-marked-faced auctioneer of watches at the fairs and festivals of Spain, who also drank too much, and two priests from Galicia who were sitting at a corner table and drinking if not too much certainly enough. At that time wine was included in the price of the room and board at the Luarca, and the waiters had just brought fresh bottles of Valdepeñas to the tables of the auctioneer, then to the picador and, finally, to the two priests.

The three waiters stood at the end of the room. It was the rule of the house that they should remain on duty until the diners whose tables they were responsible for should all have left, but the one who served the table of the two priests had an appointment to go to an Anarcho-Syndicalist meeting and Paco had agreed to take over his table for him.

Upstairs the matador who was ill was lying face down on his bed alone. The matador who was no longer a novelty was sitting looking out of his window preparatory to walking out to the café. The matador who was a coward had the older sister of Paco in his room with him and was trying to get her to do something which she was laughingly refusing to do. This matador was saying 'Come on, little savage.'

'No,' said the sister. 'Why should I?'

'For a favour.'

'You've eaten and now you want me for dessert.'

'Just once. What harm can it do?'

'Leave me alone. Leave me alone, I tell you.'

'It is a very little thing to do.'

'Leave me alone, I tell you.'

Down in the dining-room the tallest of the waiters, who was overdue at the meeting, said, 'Look at those black pigs drink.'

'That's no way to speak,' said the second waiter. 'They are decent clients. They do not drink too much.'

'For me it is a good way to speak,' said the tall one. 'There are the two curses of Spain, the bulls and the priests.'

'Certainly not the individual bull and the individual priest,' said the second waiter.

'Yes,' said the tall waiter. 'Only through the individual can you attack the class. It is necessary to kill the individual bull and the individual priest. All of them. Then there are no more.'

'Save it for the meeting,' said the other waiter.

'Look at the barbarity of Madrid,' said the tall waiter. 'It is now half past eleven o'clock and these are still guzzling.'

'They only started to eat at ten,' said the other waiter. 'As you know there are many dishes. That wine is cheap and these have paid for it. It is not a strong wine.'

'How can there be solidarity of workers with fools like you?' asked the tall waiter.

'Look,' said the second waiter who was a man of fifty. 'I have worked all my life. In all that remains of my life I must work. I have no complaints against work. To work is normal.'

'Yes, but the lack of work kills.'

'I have always worked,' said the older waiter. 'Go on to the meeting. There is no necessity to stay.'

'You are a good comrade,' said the tall waiter. 'But you lack all ideology.'

'*Mejor si me falta eso que el otro*,' said the older waiter (meaning it is better to lack that than work). 'Go on to the *mitin*.'

Paco had said nothing. He did not yet understand politics but it always gave him a thrill to hear the tall waiter speak of the necessity for killing the priests and the Guardia Civil. The tall waiter represented to him revolution and revolution also was romantic. He himself would like to be a good catholic, a revolutionary, and have a steady job like this, while, at the same time, being a bull-fighter.

'Go on to the meeting, Ignacio,' he said. 'I will respond for your work.'

'The two of us,' said the older waiter.

'There isn't enough for one,' said Paco. 'Go on to the meeting.'

'*Pues, me voy*,' said the tall waiter. 'And thanks.'

In the meantime, upstairs, the sister of Paco had gotten out of the embrace of the matador as skilfully as a wrestler breaking a hold and said, now angry, 'These are the hungry people. A failed bull-fighter. With your ton-load of fear. If you have so much of that, use it in the ring.'

'That is the way a whore talks.'

'A whore is also a woman, but I am not a whore.'

'You'll be one.'

'Not through you.'

'Leave me,' said the matador, who, now, repulsed and refused, felt the nakedness of his cowardice returning.

'Leave you? What hasn't left you?' said the sister. 'Don't you want me to make up the bed? I'm paid to do that.'

'Leave me,' said the matador, his broad good-looking face wrinkled into a contortion that was like crying. 'You whore. You dirty little whore.'

'Matador,' she said, shutting the door. 'My matador.'

Inside the room the matador sat on the bed. His face still had the contortion which, in the ring, he made into a constant smile which frightened those people in the first row of seats who knew what they were watching. 'And this,' he was saying aloud. 'And this. And this.'

He could remember when he had been good and it had only been three years before. He could remember the weight of the heavy gold-brocaded fighting jacket on his shoulders on that hot afternoon in May when his voice had still been the same in the ring as in the café, and how he sighted along the point-dipping blade at the place in the top of the shoulders where it was dusty in the short-haired black hump of muscle above the wide, wood-knocking, splintered-tipped horns that lowered as he went in to kill, and how the sword pushed in as easy as into a mound of stiff butter with the palm of his hand pushing the pommel, his left arm crossed low, his left shoulder forward, his weight on his left leg, and then his weight wasn't on his left leg. His weight was on his lower belly and as the bull raised his head the horn was out of sight in him and he swung over on it twice before they pulled him off it. So now when he went in to kill, and it was seldom, he could not look at the horns and what did any whore know about what he went through before he fought? And what had they been through that laughed at him? They were all whores and they knew what they could do with it.

Down in the dining-room the picador sat looking at the

priests. If there were women in the room he stared at them.
If there were no women he would stare with enjoyment at a
foreigner, *un inglés*, but lacking women or strangers, he now
stared with enjoyment and insolence at the two priests. While
he stared the birth-marked auctioneer rose and folding his
napkin went out, leaving over half the wine in the last bottle
he had ordered. If his accounts had been paid up at Luarca
he would have finished the bottle.

The two priests did not stare back at the picador. One of
them was saying, 'It is ten days since I have been here waiting
to see him and all day I sit in the ante-chamber and he will
not receive me.'

'What is there to do?'

'Nothing. What can one do? One cannot go against
authority.'

'I have been here for two weeks for nothing. I wait and
they will not see me.'

'We are from the abandoned country. When the money
runs out we can return.'

'To the abandoned country. What does Madrid care about
Galicia? We are a poor province.'

'One understands the action of our brother Basilio.'

'Still I have no real confidence in the integrity of Basilio
Alvarez.'

'Madrid is where one learns to understand. Madrid kills
Spain.'

'If they would simply see one and refuse.'

'No. You must be broken and worn out by waiting.'

'Well, we shall see. I can wait as well as another.'

At this moment the picador got to his feet, walked over to
the priests' table and stood, grey-headed and hawk-faced,
staring at them and smiling.

'A torero,' said one priest to the other.

'And a good one,' said the picador and walked out of the
dining-room, grey-jacketed, trim-waisted, bow-legged, in
tight breeches over his high-heeled cattleman's boots that
clicked on the floor as he swaggered quite steadily, smiling to
himself. He lived in a small, tight, professional world of

personal efficiency, nightly alcoholic triumph, and insolence. Now he lit a cigar and tilting his hat at an angle in the hallway went out to the café.

The priests left immediately after the picador, hurriedly conscious of being the last people in the dining-room, and there was no one in the room now but Paco and the middle-aged waiter. They cleared the tables and carried the bottles into the kitchen.

In the kitchen was the boy who washed the dishes. He was three years older than Paco and was very cynical and bitter.

'Take this,' the middle-aged waiter said, and poured out a glass of the Valdepeñas and handed it to him.

'Why not?' the boy took the glass.

'Tu, Paco?' the older waiter asked.

'Thank you,' said Paco. The three of them drank.

'I will be going,' said the middle-aged waiter.

'Good night,' they told him.

He went out and they were alone. Paco took a napkin one of the priests had used and standing straight, his heels planted, lowered the napkin and with head following the movement, swung his arms in the motion of a slow sweeping veronica. He turned and advancing his right foot slightly, made the second pass, gained a little terrain on the imaginary bull and made a third pass, slow, perfectly timed and suave, then gathered the napkin to his waist and swung his hips away from the bull in a media-veronica.

The dishwasher, whose name was Enrique, watched him critically and sneeringly.

'How is the bull?' he said.

'Very brave,' said Paco. 'Look.'

Standing slim and straight he made four more perfect passes, smooth, elegant and graceful.

'And the bull?' asked Enrique standing against the sink, holding his wine glass and wearing his apron.

'Still has lots of gas,' said Paco.

'You make me sick,' said Enrique.

'Why?'

'Look.'

Enrique removed his apron and citing the imaginary bull he sculptured four perfect, languid gypsy veronicas and ended up with a rebolera that made the apron swing in a stiff arc past the bull's nose as he walked away from him.

'Look at that,' he said. 'And I wash dishes.'

'Why?'

'Fear,' said Enrique. '*Miedo*. The same fear you would have in a ring with a bull.'

'No,' said Paco. 'I wouldn't be afraid.'

'*Leche!*' said Enrique. 'Everyone is afraid. But a torero can control his fear so that he can work the bull. I went in an amateur fight and I was so afraid I couldn't keep from running. Everyone thought it was very funny. So would you be afraid. If it wasn't for fear every bootblack in Spain would be a bull-fighter. You, a country boy, would be frightened worse than I was.'

'No,' said Paco.

He had done it too many times in his imagination. Too many times he had seen the horns, seen the bull's wet muzzle, the ear twitching, then the head go down and the charge, the hoofs thudding and the hot bull pass him as he swung the cape, to re-charge as he swung the cape again, then again, and again, and again, to end winding the bull around him in his great media-veronica, and walk swingingly away, with bull hairs caught in the gold ornaments of his jacket from the close passes; the bull standing hypnotized and the crowd applauding. No, he would not be afraid. Others, yes. Not he. He knew he would not be afraid. Even if he ever was afraid he knew that he could do it anyway. He had confidence. 'I wouldn't be afraid,' he said.

Enrique said, '*Leche*,' again.

Then he said, 'If we should try it?'

'How!'

'Look,' said Enrique. 'You think of the bull but you do not think of the horns. The bull has such force that the horns rip like a knife, they stab like a bayonet, and they kill like a club. Look,' he opened a table drawer and took out two meat knives. 'I will bind these to the legs of a chair. Then I will play bull for you with the chair held before my head. The knives are the horns. If you make those passes then they mean something.'

'Lend me your apron,' said Paco. 'We'll do it in the dining-room.'

'No,' said Enrique, suddenly not bitter. 'Don't do it, Paco.'

'Yes,' said Paco. 'I'm not afraid.'

'You will be when you see the knives come.'

'We'll see,' said Paco. 'Give me the apron.'

At this time, while Enrique was binding the two heavy-bladed razor-sharp meat knives fast to the legs of the chair with two soiled napkins holding the half of each knife, wrapping them tight and then knotting them, the two chambermaids, Paco's sisters, were on their way to the cinema to see Greta Garbo in 'Anna Christie'. Of the two priests, one was sitting in his underwear reading his breviary and the other was wearing a nightshirt and saying the rosary. All the bull-fighters except the one who was ill had made their evening appearance at the Café Fornos, where the big, dark-haired picador was playing billiards, the short, serious mata-dor was sitting at a crowded table before a coffee and milk, along with the middle-aged banderillero and other serious workmen.

The drinking, grey-headed picador was sitting with a glass of cazalas brandy before him staring with pleasure at a table where the matador whose courage was gone sat with another matador who had renounced the sword to become a banderillero again, and two very houseworn-looking prostitutes.

The auctioneer stood on the street corner talking with friends. The tall water was at the Anarcho-Syndicalist meeting waiting for an opportunity to speak. The middle-aged waiter was seated on the terrace of the Café Alvarez drinking a small beer. The woman who owned the Luarca was already asleep in her bed, where she lay on her back with the bolster between her legs; big, fat, honest, clean, easy-going, very religious and never having ceased to miss or pray daily for her husband, dead, now, twenty years. In his room, alone, the matador who was ill lay face down on his bed with his mouth against a handkerchief.

Now, in the deserted dining-room, Enrique tied the last knot in the napkins that bound the knives to the chair legs and lifted the chair. He pointed the legs with the knives on them forward and held the chair over his head with the two knives pointing straight ahead, one on each side of his head.

'It's heavy,' he said. 'Look, Paco. It is very dangerous. Don't do it.' He was sweating.

Paco stood facing him, holding the apron spread, holding a fold of it bunched in each hand, thumbs up, first finger down, spread to catch the eye of the bull.

'Charge straight,' he said. 'Turn like a bull. Charge as many times as you want.'

'How will you know when to cut the pass?' asked Enrique. 'It's better to do three and then a media.'

'All right,' said Paco. 'But come straight. Huh, torito! Come on, little bull!'

Running with head down Enrique came toward him and Paco swung the apron just ahead of the knife blade as it passed close in front of his belly and as it went by it was, to him, the real horn, white-tipped, black, smooth, and as Enrique passed him and turned to rush again it was the hot, blood-flanked mass of the bull that thudded by, then turned like a cat and came again as he swung the cape slowly. Then the bull turned and came again and, as he watched the on-rushing point, he stepped his left foot two inches too far forward and the knife did not pass, but had slipped in as easily as into a wineskin and there was a hot scalding rush above and around the sudden inner rigidity of steel and Enrique shouting, 'Ay! Ay! Let me get it out! Let me get it out!' and Paco slipped forward on the chair the apron cape still held, Enrique pulling on the chair as the knife turned in him, in him, Paco.

The knife was out now and he sat on the floor in the widening warm pool.

'Put the napkin over it. Hold it!' said Enrique. 'Hold it tight. I will run for the doctor. You must hold in the haemorrhage.'

'There should be a rubber cup,' said Paco. He had seen that used in the ring.

'I came straight,' said Enrique, crying. 'All I wanted was to show the danger.'

'Don't worry,' said Paco, his voice sounding far away. 'But bring the doctor.'

In the ring they lifted you and carried you, running with you, to the operating room. If the femoral artery emptied itself before you reached there they called the priest.

'Advise one of the priests,' said Paco, holding the napkin tight against his lower abdomen. He could not believe that this had happened to him.

But Enrique was running down the Carrera San Jeronimo to the all-night first-aid station and Paco was alone, first sitting up, then huddled over, then slumped on the floor, until it was over, feeling his life go out of him as dirty water empties from a bathtub when the plug is drawn. He was frightened and he felt faint and he tried to say an act of contrition and he remembered how it started but before he had said, as fast as he could, 'Oh, my God, I am heartily sorry for having offended Thee who are worthy of all my love and I firmly resolve . . .' he felt too faint and he was lying face down on the floor and it was over very quickly. A severed femoral artery empties itself faster than you can believe.

As the doctor from the first-aid station came up the stairs accompanied by a policeman who held on to Enrique by the arm, the two sisters of Paco were still in the moving-picture palace of the Gran Via, where they were intensely disappointed in the Garbo film, which showed the great star in miserable low surroundings when they had been accustomed to see her surrounded by great luxury and brilliance. The audience disliked the film thoroughly and were protesting by whistling and stamping their feet. All the other people from the hotel were doing almost what they had been doing when the accident happened, except that the two priests had finished their devotions and were preparing for sleep, and the grey-haired picador had moved his drink over to the table with the two houseworn prostitutes. A little later he went out of the café with one of them. It was the one for whom the matador who had lost his nerve had been buying drinks.

The boy Paco had never known about any of this nor about what all these people would be doing on the next day and on other days to come. He had no idea how they really lived nor how they ended. He did not even realize they ended. He died, as the Spanish phrase has it, full of illusions. He had not had time in his life to lose any of them, nor even, at the end, to complete an act of contrition.

He had not even had time to be disappointed in the Garbo picture which disappointed all Madrid for a week.

Old Man at the Bridge

An old man with steel rimmed spectacles and very dusty clothes sat by the side of the road. There was a pontoon bridge across the river and carts, trucks, and men, women and children were crossing it. The mule-drawn carts staggered up the steep bank from the bridge with soldiers helping push against the spokes of the wheels. The trucks ground up and away heading out of it all the peasants plodded along in the ankle deep dust. But the old man sat there without moving. He was too tired to go any farther.

It was my business to cross the bridge, explore the bridge-head beyond and find out to what point the enemy had advanced. I did this and returned over the bridge. There were not so many carts now and very few people on foot, but the old man was still there.

'Where do you come from?' I asked him.

'From San Carlos,' he said, and smiled.

That was his native town and so it gave him pleasure to mention it and he smiled.

'I was taking care of animals,' he explained.

'Oh,' I said, not quite understanding.

'Yes,' he said, 'I stayed, you see, taking care of animals. I was the last one to leave the town of San Carlos.'

He did not look like a shepherd nor a herdsman and I looked at his black dusty clothes and his grey dusty face and his steel rimmed spectacles and said, 'What animals were they?'

'Various animals,' he said, and shook his head. 'I had to leave them.'

I was watching the bridge and the African looking country of the Ebro Delta and wondering how long now it would be before we would see the enemy, and listening all the while for the first noises that would signal that ever mysterious event called contact, and the old man still sat there.

'What animals were they?' I asked.

'There were three animals altogether,' he explained. 'There were two goats and a cat and then there were four pairs of pigeons.'

'And you had to leave them?' I asked.

'Yes. Because of the artillery. The captain told me to go because of the artillery.'

'And you have no family?' I asked, watching the far end of the bridge where a few last carts were hurrying down the slope of the bank.

'No,' he said, 'only the animals I stated. The cat, of course, will be all right. A cat can look out for itself, but I cannot think what will become of the others.'

'What politics have you?' I asked.

'I am without politics,' he said. 'I am seventy-six years old. I have come twelve kilometres now and I think now I can go no farther.'

'This is not a good place to stop,' I said. 'If you can make it, there are trucks up the road where it forks for Tortosa.'

'I will wait a while,' he said, 'and then I will go. Where do the trucks go?'

'Towards Barcelona,' I told him.

'I know of no one in that direction,' he said, 'but thank you very much. Thank you again very much.'

He looked at me very blankly and tiredly, then said, having to share his worry with someone, 'The cat will be all right, I am sure. There is no need to be unquiet about the cat. But the others. Now what do you think about the others?'

'Why, they'll probably come through it all right.'

'You think so?'

'Why not?' I said, watching the far bank where now there were no carts.

'But what will they do under the artillery when I was told to leave because of the artillery?'

'Did you leave the dove cage unlocked?' I asked.

'Yes.'

'Then they'll fly.'

'Yes, certainly they'll fly. But the others. It's better not to think about the others,' he said.

'If you are rested I would go,' I urged. 'Get up and try to walk now.'

'Thank you,' he said and got to his feet, swayed from side to side and then sat down backwards in the dust.

'I was only taking care of animals,' he said dully, but no longer to me. 'I was only taking care of animals.'

There was nothing to do about him. It was Easter Sunday and the Fascists were advancing toward the Ebro. It was a grey overcast day with a low ceiling so their planes were not up. That and the fact that cats know how to look after themselves was all the good luck that old man would ever have.

After the Storm

It wasn't about anything, something about making punch, and then we started fighting and I slipped and he had me down kneeling on my chest and choking me with both hands like he was trying to kill me and all the time I was trying to get the knife out of my pocket to cut him loose. Everybody was too drunk to pull him off me. He was choking me and hammering my head on the floor and I got the knife out and opened it up; and I cut the muscle right across his arm and he let go of me. He couldn't have held on if he wanted to. Then he rolled and hung on to that arm and started to cry and I said:

'What the hell you want to choke me for?'

I'd have killed him. I couldn't swallow for a week. He hurt my throat bad.

Well, I went out of there and there were plenty of them with him and some came out after me and I made a turn and was down by the docks and I met a fellow and he said somebody killed a man up the street. I said, 'Who killed him?' and he said, 'I don't know who killed him but he's dead all right,' and it was dark and there was water standing in the street and no lights and windows broke and boats all up in the town and trees blown down and everything all blown and I got a skiff and went out and found my boat where I had her inside of Mango Key and she was all right only she was full of water. So I bailed her out and pumped her out and there was a moon but plenty of clouds and still plenty rough and I took it down along; and when it was daylight I was off Eastern Harbour.

Brother, that was some storm. I was the first boat out and you never saw water like that was. It was just as white as a lye barrel and coming from Eastern Harbour to Sou'west Key you couldn't recognize the shore. There was a big channel blown right out through the middle of the beach. Trees and all blown out and a channel cut through and all the water white as chalk and everything on it; branches and whole trees and dead birds, and all floating. Inside the keys were all the pelicans in the world and all kinds of birds flying. They must have gone inside there when they knew it was coming.

I lay at Sou'west Key a day and nobody came after me. I was the first boat out and I had seen a spar floating and I knew there must be a wreck and I started out to look for her. I found her. She was a three-masted schooner and I could just see the stumps of her spars out of water. She was in too deep water and I didn't get anything off of her. So I went on looking for something else. I had the start on all of them and I knew I ought to get whatever there was. I went on down over the sand-bar from where I left that three-masted schooner and I didn't find anything and I went on a long way. I was way out toward the quicksands and I didn't find anything so I went on. Then when I was in sight of the Rebecca Light I saw all kinds of birds making over something and I headed over for them to see what it was and there was a cloud of birds all right.

I could see something looked like a spar up out of the water and when I got over close the birds all went up in the air and stayed all around me. The water was clear out there and there was a spar of some kind sticking out just above the water and when I come up close to it I saw it was all dark under water like a long shadow and I came right over it and there under water was a liner; just lying there all under water as big as the whole world. I drifted over her in the boat. She lay on her side and the stern was deep down. The port holes were all shut tight and I could see the glass shine in the water and the whole of her; the biggest boat I ever saw in my life laying there and I went along the whole length of her and then I went over and anchored and I had the skiff on the deck forward and I shoved it down into the water and sculled over with the birds all around me.

I had a water glass like we use sponging and my hand shook so I could hardly hold it. All the port holes were shut that you could see along over her but way down below near the bottom something must have been open because there were pieces of things floating out all the time. You couldn't tell what they were. Just pieces. That's what the birds were after. You never saw so many birds. They were all around me; crazy yelling.

I could see everything sharp and clear. I could see her rounded over and she looked a mile long under the water. She was lying on a clear white bank of sand and the spar was a sort of foremast or some sort of tackle that slanted out of the water the way she was laying on her side. Her bow wasn't very far under. I could stand on the letters of her name on her bow and my head was just out of water. But the nearest port hole was twelve feet down. I could just reach it with the grains pole and I tried to break it with that but I couldn't. The glass was too stout. So I sculled back to the boat, and got a wrench and lashed it to the end of the grains pole and I couldn't break it. There I was looking down through the glass at that liner with everything in her and I was the first one to her and I couldn't get into her. She must have had five million dollars' worth in her.

It made me shake to think how much she must have in her. Inside the port hole that was closed I could see something but I couldn't make it out through the water glass. I couldn't do any good with the grains pole and I took off my clothes and stood and took a couple of deep breaths and dove over off the stern with the wrench in my hand and swam down. I could hold on for a second to the edge of the port hole, and I could see in and there was a woman inside with her hair floating all out. I could see her floating plain and I hit the glass twice with the wrench hard and I heard the noise clink in my ears but it wouldn't break and I had to come up.

I hung on to the dinghy and got my breath and then I climbed in and took of couple of breaths and dove again. I swam down and took hold of the edge of the port hole with my fingers and held it and hit the glass as hard as I could with the wrench. I could see the woman floated in the water through the glass. Her hair was tied once close to her head and it floated all out in the water. I could see the rings on one of her hands. She was right up close to the port hole and I hit the glass twice and I didn't even crack it. When I came up I thought I wouldn't make it to the top before I'd have to breathe.

I went down once more and I cracked the glass, only cracked it, and when I came up my nose was bleeding and I stood on the bow of the liner with my bare feet in the letters of her name and my head just out and rested there and then I swam over to the skiff and pulled up into it and sat there waiting for my head to stop aching and looking down into the water glass, but I bled so I had to wash out the water glass. Then I lay back in the skiff and held my hand under my nose to stop it and I lay there with my head back looking up and there was a million birds above and all around.

When I quit bleeding I took another look through the glass and then I sculled over to the boat to try and find something heavier than the wrench but I couldn't find a thing; not even a sponge hook. I went back and the water was clearer all the time and you could see everything that floated out over that white bank of sand. I looked for sharks but there weren't any. You could have seen a shark a long way away. The water was so clear and the sand white. There was a grapple for an anchor on the skiff and I cut it off and went overboard and down with it. It carried me right down and past the port hole and I grabbed and couldn't hold anything and went on down and down, sliding along the curved side of her. I had to let go of the grapple. I heard it bump once and it seemed like a year before I came up through to the top of the water. The skiff was floated away with the tide and I swam over to her with my nose bleeding in the water while I swam and I was plenty glad there weren't sharks; but I was tired.

My head felt cracked open and I lay in the skiff and rested and then sculled back. It was getting along in the afternoon. I went down once more with the wrench and it didn't do any good. That wrench was too light. It wasn't any good diving unless you had a big hammer or something heavy enough to do good. Then I lashed the wrench to the grains pole again and I watched through the water glass and pounded on the glass and hammered until the wrench came off and I saw it in the glass, clear and sharp, go sliding down along her and then off and down to the quicksand and go in. Then I couldn't do a thing. The wrench was gone and I'd lost the grapple so I sculled back to the boat. I was too tired to get the skiff aboard and the sun was pretty low. The birds were all pulling out and leaving her and I headed for Sou'west Key towing the skiff and the birds going on ahead of me and behind me. I was plenty tired.

That night it came on to blow and it blew for a week. You couldn't get out to her. They come out from town and told me the fellow I'd had to cut was all right except for his arm and I went back to town and they put me under five hundred dollar bond. It came out all right because some of them, friends of mine, swore he was after me with an axe, but by the time we got back out to her the Greeks had blown her open and cleaned her out. They got the safe out with dynamite. Nobody ever knows how much they got. She carried gold and they got it all. They stripped her clean. I found her and I never got a nickel out of her.

It was a hell of a thing all right. They say she was just outside of Havana harbour when the hurricane hit and she couldn't get in or the owners wouldn't let the captain chance coming in; they say he wanted to try; so she had to go with it and in the dark they were running with it trying to go through the gulf between Rebecca and Tortugas when she struck on the quicksands. Maybe her rudder was carried away. Maybe they weren't even steering. But anyway they couldn't have known they were quicksands and when she struck the captain must have ordered them to open up the ballast tanks so she'd lay solid. But it was quicksand she'd hit and when they opened the tank she went in stern first and then over on her beam ends. There were four hundred and fifty passengers and the crew on board of her and they must all have been aboard of her when I found her. They must have opened the tanks as soon as she struck and the minute she settled on it the quicksands took her down. Then her boilers must have burst and that must have been what made those pieces that came out. It was funny there weren't any sharks though. There wasn't a fish. I could have seen them on that clear white sand.

Plenty of fish now though; jewfish, the biggest kind. The biggest part of her's under the sand now but they live inside of her; the biggest kind of jewfish. Some weigh three to four hundred pounds. Sometime we'll go out and get some. You can see the Rebecca light from where she is. They've got a buoy on her now. She's right at the end of the quicksand right at the edge of the gulf. She only missed going through by about a hundred yards. In the dark in the storm they just missed it; raining the way it was they couldn't have seen the Rebecca. Then they're not used to that sort of thing. The captain of a liner isn't used to scudding that way. They have a course and they tell me they set some sort of a compass and it steers itself. They probably didn't know where they were when they ran with that blow but they came close to making it. Maybe they'd lost the rudder though. Anyway there wasn't another thing for them to hit till they'd get to Mexico once they were in that gulf. Must have been something though when they struck in that rain and wind and he told them to open her tanks. Nobody could have been on deck in that blow and rain. Everybody must have been below. They couldn't have lived on deck. There must have been some scenes inside all right because you know she settled fast. I saw that wrench go into the sand. The captain couldn't have known it was quicksand when she struck unless he knew these waters. He just knew it wasn't rock. He must have seen it all up in the bridge. He must have known what it was about when she settled. I wonder how fast she made it. I wonder if the mate was there with him. Do you think they stayed inside the bridge or do you think they took it outside? They never found any bodies. Not a one. Nobody floating. They float a long way with lifebelts too. They must have took it inside. Well, the Greeks got it all. Everything. They must have come fast all right. They picked her clean. First there was the birds, then me, then the Greeks, and even the birds got more out of her than I did.

A Clean, Well-Lighted Place

It was late and everyone had left the café except an old man who sat in the shadow the leaves of the tree made against the electric light. In the daytime the street was dusty, but at night the dew settled the dust and the old man liked to sit late because he was deaf and now at night it was quiet and he felt the difference. The two waiters inside the café knew that the old man was a little drunk, and while he was a good client they knew that if he became too drunk he would leave without paying, so they kept watch on him.

'Last week he tried to commit suicide,' one waiter said.

'Why?'

'He was in despair.'

'What about?'

'Nothing.'

'How do you know it was nothing?'

'He has plenty of money.'

They sat together at a table that was close against the wall near the door of the café and looked at the terrace where the tables were all empty except where the old man sat in the shadow of the leaves of the tree that moved slightly in the wind. A girl and a soldier went by in the street. The street light shone on the brass number on his collar. The girl wore no head covering and hurried beside him.

'The guard will pick him up,' one waiter said.

'What does it matter if he gets what he's after?'

'He had better get off the street now. The guard will get him. They went by five minutes ago.'

The old man sitting in the shadow rapped on his saucer with his glass. The younger waiter went over to him.

'What do you want?'

The old man looked at him. 'Another brandy,' he said.

'You'll be drunk,' the waiter said. The old man looked at him. The waiter went away.

'He'll stay all night,' he said to his colleague. 'I'm sleepy now. I never get to bed before three o'clock. He should have killed himself last week.'

The waiter took the brandy bottle and another saucer from the counter inside the café and marched out to the old man's table. He put down the saucer and poured the glass full of brandy.

'You should have killed yourself last week,' he said to the deaf man. The old man motioned with his finger. 'A little more,' he said. The waiter poured on into the glass so that the brandy slopped over and ran down the stem into the top saucer of the pile. 'Thank you,' the old man said. The waiter took the bottle back inside the café. He sat down at the table with his colleague again.

'He's drunk now,' he said.

'He's drunk every night.'

'What did he want to kill himself for?'

'How should I know?'

'How did he do it?'

'He hung himself with a rope.'

'Who cut him down?'

'His niece.'

'Why did they do it?'

'Fear for his soul.'

'How much money has he got?'

'He's got plenty.'

'He must be eighty years old.'

'Anyway I should say he was eighty.'

'I wish he would go home. I never get to bed before three o'clock. What kind of hour is that to go to bed?'

'He stays up because he likes it.'

'He's lonely. I'm not lonely. I have a wife waiting in bed for me.'

'He had a wife once too.'

'A wife would be no good to him now.'

'You can't tell. He might be better with a wife.'

'His niece looks after him.'

'I know. You said she cut him down.'

'I wouldn't want to be that old. An old man is a nasty thing.'

'Not always. This old man is clean. He drinks without spilling. Even now, drunk. Look at him.'

'I don't want to look at him. I wish he would go home. He has no regard for those who must work.'

The old man looked from his glass across the square, then over at the waiters.

'Another brandy,' he said, pointing to his glass. The waiter who was in a hurry came over.

'Finished,' he said, speaking with that omission of syntax stupid people employ when talking to drunken people or foreigners. 'No more tonight. Close now.'

'Another,' said the old man.

'No. Finished.' The waiter wiped the edge of the table with a towel and shook his head.

The old man stood up, slowly counted the saucers, took a leather coin purse from his pocket and paid for the drinks, leaving half a peseta tip.

The waiter watched him go down the street, a very old man walking unsteadily but with dignity.

'Why didn't you let him stay and drink?' the unhurried waiter asked. They were putting up the shutters. 'It is not half past two.'

'I want to go home to bed.'

'What is an hour?'

'More to me than to him.'

'An hour is the same.'

'You talk like an old man yourself. He can buy a bottle and drink at home.'

'It's not the same.'

'No, it is not,' agreed the waiter with a wife. He did not wish to be unjust. He was only in a hurry.

'And you? You have no fear of going home before your usual hour?'

'Are you trying to insult me?'

'No, hombre, only to make a joke.'

'No,' the waiter who was in a hurry said, rising from pulling down the metal shutters. 'I have confidence. I am all confidence.'

'You have youth, confidence, and a job,' the older waiter said. 'You have everything.'

'And what do you lack?'

'Everything but work.'

'You have everything I have.'

'No. I have never had confidence and I am not young.'

'Come on. Stop talking nonsense and lock up.'

'I am of those who like to stay late at the café,' the older waiter said. 'With all those who do not want to go to bed. With all those who need a light for the night.'

'I want to go home and into bed.'

'We are of two different kinds,' the older waiter said. He was dressed now to go home. 'It is not only a question of youth and confidence, although those things are very beautiful. Each night I am reluctant to close up because there may be someone who needs the café.'

'Hombre, there are bodegas open all night long.'

'You do not understand. This is a clean and pleasant café. It is well lighted. The light is very good and also, now, there are shadows of the leaves.'

'Good night,' said the younger waiter.

'Good night,' the other said. Turning off the electric light he continued the conversation with himself. It is the light of course but it is necessary that the place be clean and pleasant. You do not want music. Certainly you do not want music. Nor can you stand before a bar with dignity although that is all that is provided for these hours. What did he fear? It was not fear or dread. It was a nothing that he knew too well. It was all a nothing and a man was nothing too. It was only that and light was all it needed and a certain cleanness and order. Some lived in it and never felt it but he knew it all was nada y pues nada y nada y pues nada. Our nada who art in nada, nada be thy name thy kingdom nada thy will be nada in nada as it is in nada. Give us this nada our daily nada and nada us our nada as we nada our nadas and nada us not into nada but deliver us from nada; pues nada. Hail nothing full of nothing, nothing is with thee. He smiled and stood before a bar with a shining steam pressure coffee machine.

'What's yours?' asked the barman.

'Nada.'

'Otro loco mas,' said the barman and turned away.

'A little cup,' said the waiter.

The barman poured it for him.

'The light is very bright and pleasant but the bar is unpolished,' the waiter said.

The barman looked at him but did not answer. It was too late at night for conversation.

'You want another copita?' the barman asked.

'No, thank you,' said the waiter and went out. He disliked bars and bodegas. A clean, well-lighted café was a very different thing. Now, without thinking further, he would go home to his room. He would lie in the bed and finally, with daylight, he would go to sleep. After all, he said to himself, it is probably only insomnia. Many must have it.

The Light of the World

When he saw us come in the door the bartender looked up and then reached over and put the glass covers on the two free-lunch bowls.

'Give me a beer,' I said. He drew it, cut the top off with the spatula and then held the glass in his hand. I put the nickel on the wood and he slid the beer toward me.

'What's yours?' he said to Tom.

'Beer.'

He drew that beer and cut it off and when he saw the money he pushed the beer across to Tom.

'What's the matter?' Tom asked.

The bartender didn't answer him. He just looked over our heads and said, 'What's yours?' to a man who'd come in.

'Rye,' the man said. The bartender put out the bottle and glass and a glass of water.

Tom reached over and took the glass off the free-lunch bowl. It was a bowl of pickled pigs' feet and there was a wooden thing that worked like a scissors, with two wooden forks at the end to pick them up with.

'No,' said the bartender and put the glass cover back on the bowl. Tom held the wooden scissors fork in his hand. 'Put it back,' said the bartender.

'You know where,' said Tom.

The bartender reached a hand forward under the bar, watching us both. I put fifty cents on the wood and he straightened up.

'What was yours?' he said.

'Beer,' I said, and before he drew the beer he uncovered both the bowls.

'Your goddam pig's feet stink,' Tom said, and spit what he had in his mouth on the floor. The bartender didn't say anything. The man who had drunk the rye paid and went out without looking back.

'You stink yourself,' the bartender said. 'All you punks stink.'

'He says we're punks,' Tommy said to me.

'Listen,' I said. 'Let's get out.'

'You punks clear the hell out of here,' the bartender said.

'I said we were going out,' I said. 'It wasn't your idea.'

'We'll be back,' Tommy said.

'No you won't,' the bartender told him.

'Tell him how wrong he is,' Tom turned to me.

'Come on,' I said.

Outside it was good and dark.

'What the hell kind of place is this?' Tommy said.

'I don't know,' I said. 'Let's go down to the station.'

We'd come in that town at one end and we were going out the other. It smelled of hides and tan bark and the big piles of sawdust. It was getting dark as we came in, and now that it was dark it was cold and the puddles of water in the road were freezing at the edges.

Down at the station there were five whores waiting for the train to come in, and six white men and four Indians. It was crowded and hot from the stove and full of stale smoke. As we came in nobody was talking and the ticket window was down.

'Shut the door, can't you!' somebody said.

I looked to see who said it. It was one of the white men. He wore stagged trousers and lumbermen's rubbers and a mackinaw shirt like the others, but he had no cap and his face was white and his hands were white and thin.

'Aren't you going to shut it?'

'Sure,' I said, and shut it.

'Thank you,' he said. One of the other men snickered.

'Ever interfere with a cook?' he said to me.

'No.'

'You can interfere with this one,' he looked at the cook. 'He likes it.'

The cook looked away from him holding his lips tight together.

'He puts lemon juice on his hands,' the man said. 'He

wouldn't get them in dishwater for anything. Look how white they are.'

One of the whores laughed out loud. She was the biggest whore I ever saw in my life and the biggest woman. And she had on one of those silk dresses that change colours. There were two other whores that were nearly as big but the big one must have weighed three hundred and fifty pounds. You couldn't believe she was real when you looked at her. All three had those changeable silk dresses. They sat side by side on the bench. They were huge. The other two were just ordinary looking whores, peroxide blondes.

'Look at his hands,' the man said and nodded his head at the cook. The whore laughed again and shook all over.

The cook turned and said to her quickly. 'You big disgusting mountain of flesh.'

She just kept on laughing and shaking.

'Oh, my Christ,' she said. She had a nice voice. 'Oh, my sweet Christ.'

The other two whores, the big ones, acted very quiet and placid as though they didn't have much sense, but they were big, nearly as big as the biggest one. They'd have both gone well over two hundred and fifty pounds. The other two were dignified.

Of the men, besides the cook and the one who talked, there were two other lumberjacks, one that listened, interested but bashful, and the other that seemed getting ready to say something, and two Swedes. Two Indians were sitting down at the end of the bench and one standing up against the wall.

The man who was getting ready to say something spoke to me very low. 'Must be like getting on top of a hay mow.'

I laughed and said it to Tommy.

'I swear to Christ I've never been anywhere like this,' he said. 'Look at the three of them.' Then the cook spoke up.

'How old are you boys?'

'I'm ninety-six and he's sixty-nine,' Tommy said.

'Ho! Ho! Ho!' the big whore shook with laughing. She had a really pretty voice. The other whores didn't smile.

'Oh, can't you be decent?' the cook said. 'I asked just to be friendly.'

'We're seventeen and nineteen,' I said.

'What's the matter with you?' Tommy turned to me.

'That's all right.'

'You can call me Alice,' the big whore said and then she began to shake again.

'Is that your name?' Tommy asked.

'Sure,' she said. 'Alice. Isn't it?' she turned to the man who sat by the cook.

'Alice. That's right.'

'That's the sort of name you'd have,' the cook said.

'It's my real name,' Alice said.

'What's the other girls' names?' Tom asked.

'Hazel and Ethel,' Alice said. Hazel and Ethel smiled. They weren't very bright.

'What's your name?' I said to one of the blondes.

'Frances,' she said.

'Frances Wilson. What's it to you?'

'What's yours?' I asked the other one.

'Oh, don't be fresh,' she said.

'He just wants us all to be friends,' the man who talked said. 'Don't you want to be friends?'

'No,' the peroxide one said. 'Not with you.'

'She's just a spitfire,' the man said. 'A regular little spitfire.'

The one blonde looked at the other and shook her head.

'Goddamned mossbacks,' she said.

Alice commenced to laugh again and to shake all over.

'There's nothing funny,' the cook said. 'You all laugh but there's nothing funny. You two young lads; where are you bound for?'

'Where are you going yourself?' Tom asked him.

'I want to go to Cadillac,' the cook said. 'Have you ever been there? My sister lives there.'

'He's a sister himself,' the man in the stagged trousers said.

'Can't you stop that sort of thing?' the cook asked. 'Can't we speak decently?'

'Cadillac is where Steve Ketchel came from and where Ad Wolgast is from,' the shy man said.

'Steve Ketchel,' one of the blondes said in a high voice as though the name had pulled a trigger in her. 'His own father shot and killed him. Yes, by Christ, his own father. There aren't any more men like Steve Ketchel.'

'Wasn't his name Stanley Ketchel?' asked the cook.

'Oh, shut up,' said the blonde. 'What do you know about Steve? Stanley. He was no Stanley. Steve Ketchel was the finest and most beautiful man that ever lived. I never saw a man as clean and as white and as beautiful as Steve Ketchel. There never was a man like that. He moved just like a tiger and he was the finest, free-est spender that ever lived.'

'Did you know him?' one of the men asked.

'Did I know him? Did I know him? Did I love him? You ask me that? I knew him like you know nobody in the world and I loved him like you love God. He was the greatest, finest, whitest, most beautiful man that ever lived, Steve Ketchel, and his own father shot him down like a dog.'

'Were you out on the coast with him?'

'No. I knew him before that. He was the only man I ever loved.'

Everyone was very respectful to the peroxide blonde, who said all this in a high stagey way, but Alice was beginning to shake again. I felt it sitting by her.

'You should have married him,' the cook said.

'I wouldn't hurt his career,' the peroxide blonde said. 'I wouldn't be a drawback to him. A wife wasn't what he needed. Oh, my God, what a man he was.'

'That was a fine way to look at it,' the cook said. 'Didn't Jack Johnson knock him out though?'

'It was a trick,' Peroxide said. 'That big dinge took him by surprise. He'd just knocked Jack Johnson down, the big black bastard. That nigger beat him by a fluke.'

The ticket window went up and the three Indians went over to it.

'Steve knocked him down,' Peroxide said. 'He turned to smile at me.'

'I thought you said you weren't on the coast,' someone said.

'I went out just for that fight. Steve turned to smile at me and that black son of a bitch from hell jumped up and hit him by surprise. Steve could lick a hundred like that black bastard.'

'He was a great fighter,' the lumberjack said.

'I hope to God he was,' Peroxide said. 'I hope to God they don't have fighters like that now. He was like a god, he was. So white and clean and beautiful and smooth and fast and like a tiger or like lightning.'

'I saw him in the moving pictures of the fight,' Tom said. We were all very moved. Alice was shaking all over and I looked and saw she was crying. The Indians had gone outside on the platform.

'He was more than any husband could ever be,' Peroxide said. 'We were married in the eyes of God and I belong to him right now and always will and all of me is his. I don't care about my body. They can take my body. My soul belongs to Steve Ketchel. By God, he was a man.'

Everybody felt terribly. It was sad and embarrassing. Then Alice, who was still shaking, spoke. 'You're a dirty liar,' she said in that low voice. 'You never layed Steve Ketchel in your life and you know it.'

'How can you say that?' Peroxide said proudly.

'I say it because it's true,' Alice said. 'I'm the only one here that ever knew Steve Ketchel and I come from Mancelona and I knew him there and it's true and you know it's true and God can strike me dead if it isn't true.'

'He can strike me too,' Peroxide said.

'This is true, true, true, and you know it. Not just made up and I know exactly what he said to me.'

'What did he say?' Peroxide asked, complacently.

Alice was crying so she could hardly speak from shaking so. 'He said, "You're a lovely piece, Alice." That's exactly what he said.'

'It's a lie,' Peroxide said.

'It's true,' Alice said. 'That's truly what he said.'

'It's a lie,' Peroxide said proudly.

'No, it's true, true, true, to Jesus and Mary true.'

'Steve couldn't have said that. It wasn't the way he talked,' Peroxide said happily.

'It's true,' said Alice in her nice voice. 'And it doesn't make any difference to me whether you believe it or not.' She wasn't crying any more and she was calm.

'It would be impossible for Steve to have said that,' Peroxide declared.

'He said it,' Alice said and smiled. 'And I remember when he said it and I *was* a lovely piece then exactly as he said, and right now I'm a better piece than you, you dried-up old hot water-bottle.'

'You can't insult me,' said Peroxide. 'You big mountain of pus. I have my memories.'

'No,' Alice said in that sweet lovely voice, 'you haven't got any real memories except having your tubes out and when you started C. and M. Everything else you just read in the papers. I'm clean and you know it, and men like me, even though I'm big, and you know it, and I never lie and you know it.'

'Leave me with my memories,' Peroxide said. 'With my true, wonderful memories.'

Alice looked at her and then at us and her face lost that hurt look and she smiled and she had the prettiest face I ever saw. She had a pretty face and a nice smooth skin and a lovely voice and she was nice all right and really friendly. But my God she was big. She was big as three women. Tom saw me looking at her and he said, 'Come on. Let's go.'

'Good-bye,' said Alice. She certainly had a nice voice.

'Good-bye,' I said.

'Which way are you boys going?' asked the cook.

'The other way from you,' Tom told him.

God Rest You Merry, Gentlemen

In those days the distances were all very different, the dirt blew off the hills that now have been cut down, and Kansas City was very like Constantinople. You may not believe this. No one believes this; but it is true. On this afternoon it was snowing and inside an automobile dealer's show window, lighted against the early dark, there was a racing motor car finished entirely in silver with Dans Argent lettered on the hood. This I believed to mean the silver dance or the silver dancer, and, slightly puzzled which it meant but happy in the sight of the car and pleased by my knowledge of a foreign language, I went along the street in the snow. I was walking from the Woolf Brothers' saloon where, on Christmas and Thanksgiving Day, a free turkey dinner was served, toward the city hospital which was on a high hill that overlooked the smoke, the buildings and the streets of the town. In the reception room of the hospital were the two ambulance surgeons, Doc Fischer and Doctor Wilcox, sitting, the one before a desk, the other in a chair against the wall.

Doc Fischer was thin, sand-blond, with a thin mouth, amused eyes and gambler's hands. Doctor Wilcox was short, dark and carried an indexed book, *The Young Doctor's Friend and Guide*, which, being consulted on any given subject, told symptoms and treatment. It was also cross-indexed so that being consulted on symptoms it gave diagnoses. Doc Fischer had suggested that any future editions should be further cross-indexed so that if consulted as to the treatments being given, it would reveal ailments and symptoms. 'As an aid to memory,' he said.

Doctor Wilcox was sensitive about this book but could not get along without it. It was bound in limp leather and fitted his coat pocket and he had bought it at the advice of one of his professors who had said, 'Wilcox, you have no business being a physician and I have done everything in my power to prevent you from being certified as one. Since you are now a

74

member of this learned profession I advise you, in the name of humanity, to obtain a copy of *The Young Doctor's Friend and Guide*, and use it, Doctor Wilcox. Learn to use it.'

Doctor Wilcox had said nothing but he had bought the leather-bound guide that same day.

'Well, Horace,' Doc Fischer said as I came in the receiving room which smelt of cigarettes, iodoform, carbolic and an over-heated radiator.

'Gentlemen,' I said.

'What news along the rialto?' Doc Fischer asked. He affected a certain extravagance of speech which seemed to me to be of the utmost elegance.

'The free turkey at Woolf's,' I answered.

'You partook?'

'Copiously.'

'Many of the confrères present?'

'All of them. The whole staff.'

'Much Yuletide cheer?'

'Not much.'

'Doctor Wilcox here has partaken slightly,' Doc Fischer said. Doctor Wilcox looked up at him, then at me.

'Want a drink?' he asked.

'No, thanks,' I said.

'That's all right,' Doctor Wilcox said.

'Horace,' Doc Fischer said, 'you don't mind me calling you Horace, do you?'

'No.'

'Good old Horace. We've had an extremely interesting case.'

'I'll say,' said Doctor Wilcox.

'You know the lad who was in here yesterday?'

'Which one?'

'The lad who sought eunuch-hood.'

'Yes.' I had been there when he came in. He was a boy about sixteen. He came in with no hat on and was very excited and frightened but determined. He was curly haired and well built and his lips were prominent.

'What's the matter with you, son?' Doctor Wilcox asked him.

'I want to be castrated,' the boy said.

'Why?' Doc Fischer asked.

'I've prayed and I've done everything and nothing helps.'

'Helps what?'

'That awful lust.'

'What awful lust?'

'The way I get. That way I can't stop getting. I pray all night about it.'

'Just what happens?' Doc Fischer asked.

The boy told him. 'Listen, boy,' Doc Fischer said. 'There's nothing wrong with you. That's the way you're supposed to be. There's nothing wrong with that.'

'It is wrong,' said the boy. 'It's a sin against purity. It's a sin against our Lord and Saviour.'

'No,' said Doc Fischer. 'It's a natural thing. It's the way you are supposed to be and later on you will think you are very fortunate.'

'Oh, you don't understand,' the boy said.

'Listen,' Doc Fischer said and he told the boy certain things.

'No. I won't listen. You can't make me listen.'

'Please listen,' Doc Fischer said.

'You're just a goddamned fool,' Doctor Wilcox said to the boy.

'Then you won't do it?' the boy asked.

'Do what?'

'Castrate me.'

'Listen,' Doc Fischer said. 'No one will castrate you. There is nothing wrong with your body. You have a fine body and you must not think about that. If you are religious remember that what you complain of is no sinful state but the means of consummating a sacrament.'

'I can't stop it happening,' the boy said. 'I pray all night and I pray in the daytime. It is a sin, a constant sin against purity.'

'Oh, go and –' Doctor Wilcox said.

'When you talk like that I don't hear you,' the boy said with dignity to Doctor Wilcox. 'Won't you please do it?' he asked Doc Fischer.

'No,' said Doc Fischer. 'I've told you, boy.'

'Get him out of here,' Doctor Wilcox said.

That was about five o'clock on the day before.

'So what happened?' I asked.

'So at one o'clock this morning,' Doc Fischer said, 'we receive the youth self-mutilated with a razor.'

'Castrated?'

'No,' said Doc Fischer. 'He didn't know what castrate meant.'

'He may die,' Doctor Wilcox said.

'Why?'

'Loss of blood.'

'The good physician here, Doctor Wilcox, my colleague, was on call and he was unable to find this emergency listed in his book.'

'The hell with you talking that way,' Doctor Wilcox said.

'I only mean it in the friendliest way, Doctor,' Doc Fischer said, looking at his hands, at his hands that had, with his willingness to oblige and his lack of respect for Federal statutes, made him his trouble. 'Horace here will bear me out that I only speak of it in the very friendliest way. It was an amputation the young man performed, Horace.'

'Well, I wish you wouldn't ride me about it,' Doctor Wilcox said. 'There isn't any need to ride me.'

'Ride you, Doctor, on the day, the very anniversary, of our Saviour's birth?'

'*Our* Saviour? Ain't you a Jew?' Doctor Wilcox said.

'So I am. So I am. It always is slipping my mind. I've never given it its proper importance. So good of you to remind me. *Your* Saviour. That's right. *Your* Saviour, undoubtedly *your* Saviour – and the ride for Palm Sunday.'

'You're too damned smart,' Doctor Wilcox said.

'An excellent diagnosis, Doctor. I was always too damned smart. Too damned smart on the coast certainly. Avoid it, Horace. You haven't much tendency but sometimes I see a gleam. But what a diagnosis – and without the book.'

'The hell with you,' Doctor Wilcox said.

'All in good time, Doctor,' Doc Fischer said. 'All in good time. If there is such a place I shall certainly visit it. I have even had a very small look into it. No more than a peek, really. I looked away almost at once. And do you know what the young man said, Horace, when the good Doctor here brought him in? He said, "Oh, I asked you to do it. I asked you so many times to do it." '

'On Christmas Day, too,' Doctor Wilcox said.

'The significance of the particular day is not important,' Doc Fischer said.

'Maybe not to you,' said Doctor Wilcox.

'You hear him, Horace?' Doc Fischer said. 'You hear him? Having discovered my vulnerable point, my achilles tendon, so to speak, the doctor pursues his advantage.'

'You're too damned smart,' Doctor Wilcox said.

The Sea Change

'All right,' said the man. 'What about it?'

'No,' said the girl. 'I can't.'

'You mean you won't.'

'I can't,' said the girl. 'That's all that I mean.'

'You mean that you won't.'

'All right,' said the girl. 'You have it your own way.'

'I don't have it my own way. I wish to God I did.'

'You did for a long time,' the girl said.

It was early, and there was no one in the café except the barman and these two who sat together at a table in the corner. It was the end of the summer and they were both tanned, so that they looked out of place in Paris. The girl wore a tweed suit, her skin was a smooth golden brown, her blonde hair was cut short and grew beautifully away from her forehead. The man looked at her.

'I'll kill her,' he said.

'Please don't,' the girl said. She had very fine hands and the man looked at them. They were slim and brown and very beautiful.

'I will. I swear to God I will.'

'It won't make you happy.'

'Couldn't you have gotten into something else? Couldn't you have gotten into some other jam?'

'It seems not,' the girl said. 'What are you going to do about it?'

'I told you.'

'No; I mean really.'

'I don't know,' he said. She looked at him and put out her hand. 'Poor old Phil,' she said. He looked at her hands, but he did not touch her hand with his.

'No, thanks,' he said.

'It doesn't do any good to say I'm sorry?'

'No.'

'Nor to tell you how it is?'

79

'I'd rather not hear.'

'I love you very much.'

'Yes, this proves it.'

'I'm sorry,' she said, 'if you don't understand.'

'I understand. That's the trouble. I understand.'

'You do,' she said. 'That makes it worse, of course.'

'Sure,' he said, looking at her. 'I'll understand all the time. All day and all night. Especially at night. I'll understand. You don't have to worry about that.'

'I'm sorry,' she said.

'If it was a man –'

'Don't say that. It wouldn't be a man. You know that. Don't you trust me?'

'That's funny,' he said. 'Trust you. That's really funny.'

'I'm sorry,' she said. 'That's all I seem to say. But when we do understand each other there's no use to pretend we don't.'

'No,' he said. 'I suppose not.'

'I'll come back if you want me.'

'No. I don't want you.'

Then they did not say anything for a while.

'You don't believe I love you, do you?' the girl asked.

'Let's not talk rot,' the man said.

'Don't you really believe I love you?'

'Why don't you prove it?'

'You didn't used to be that way. You never asked me to prove anything. That isn't polite.'

'You're a funny girl.'

'You're not. You're a fine man and it breaks my heart to go off and leave you –'

'You have to, of course.'

'Yes,' she said. 'I have to and you know it.'

He did not say anything and she looked at him and put her hand out again. The barman was at the far end of the bar. His face was white and so was his jacket. He knew these two and thought them a handsome young couple. He had seen many handsome young couples break up and new couples form that were never so handsome long. He was not thinking about this, but about a horse. In half an hour he could send across the street to find if the horse had won.

'Couldn't you just be good to me and let me go?' the girl asked.

'What do you think I'm going to do?'

Two people came in the door and went up to the bar.

'Yes, sir,' the barman took the orders.

'You can't forgive me? When you know about it?' the girl asked.

'No.'

'You don't think things we've had and done should make any difference in understanding?'

' "Vice is a monster of such fearful mien," ' the young man said bitterly, 'that to be something or other needs but to be seen. Then we something, something, then embrace.' He could not remember the words. 'I can't quote,' he said.

'Let's not say vice,' she said. 'That's not very polite.'

'Perversion,' he said.

'James,' one of the clients addressed the barman, 'you're looking very well.'

'You're looking very well yourself,' the barman said.

'Old James,' the other client said. 'You're better, James.'

'It's terrible,' the barman said, 'the way I put it on.'

'Don't neglect to insert the brandy, James,' the first client said.

'No, sir,' said the barman. 'Trust me.'

The two at the bar looked over at the two at the table, then looked back at the barman again. Toward the barman was the comfortable direction.

'I'd like it better if you didn't use words like that,' the girl said. 'There's no necessity to use a word like that.'

'What do you want me to call it?'

'You don't have to call it. You don't have to put any name to it.'

'That's the name for it.'

'No,' she said. 'We're made up of all sorts of things. You've known that. You've used it well enough.'

'You don't have to say that again.'

'Because that explains it to you.'

'All right,' he said. 'All right.'

'You mean all wrong. I know. It's all wrong. But I'll come back. I told you I'd come back. I'll come back right away.'

'No, you won't.'

'I'll come back.'

'No, you won't. Not to me.'

'You'll see.'

'Yes,' he said. 'That's the hell of it. You probably will.'

'Of course I will.'

'Go on, then.'

'Really?' She could not believe him, but her voice was happy.

'Go on,' his voice sounded strange to him. He was looking at her, at the way her mouth went and the curve of her cheek-bones, at her eyes and at the way her hair grew on her forehead and at the edge of her ear and at her neck.

'Not really. Oh, you're too sweet,' she said. 'You're too good to me.'

'And when you come back tell me all about it.' His voice sounded very strange. He did not recognize it. She looked at him quickly. He was settled into something.

'You want me to go?' she asked seriously.

'Yes,' he said seriously. 'Right away.' His voice was not the same, and his mouth was very dry. 'Now,' he said.

She stood up and went out quickly. She did not look back at him. He watched her go. He was not the same-looking man as he had been before he had told her to go. He got up from the table, picked up the two checks and went over to the bar with them.

'I'm a different man, James,' he said to the barman. 'You see in me quite a different man.'

'Yes, sir?' said James.

'Vice,' said the brown young man, 'is a very strange thing, James.' He looked out the door. He saw her going down the street. As he looked in the glass, he saw he was really quite a different-looking man. The other two at the bar moved down to make room for him.

'You're right there, sir,' James said.

The other two moved down a little more, so that he would be quite comfortable. The young man saw himself in the mirror behind the bar. 'I said I was a different man, James,' he said. Looking into the mirror he saw that this was quite true.

'You look very well, sir,' James said. 'You must have had a very good summer.'

A Way You'll Never Be

The attack had gone across the field, been held up by machine-gun fire from the sunken road and from the group of farm houses, encountered no resistance in the town, and reached the bank of the river. Coming along the road on a bicycle, getting off to push the machine when the surface of the road became too broken, Nicholas Adams saw what had happened by the position of the dead.

They lay alone or in clumps in the high grass of the fields and along the road, their pockets out, and over them were flies and around each body or group of bodies were the scattered papers.

In the grass and the grain, beside the road, and in some places scattered over the road, there was much material: a field kitchen, it must have come over when things were going well; many of the calf-skin-covered haversacks, stick bombs, helmets, rifles, sometimes one butt-up, the bayonets stuck in the dirt, they had dug quite a little at the last; stick bombs, helmets, rifles, entrenching tools, ammunition boxes, starshell pistols, their shells scattered about, medical kits, gas masks, empty gas mask cans, a squat, tripodded machine-gun in a nest of empty shells, full belts protruding from the boxes, the water-cooling can empty and on its side, the breech block gone, the crew in odd positions, and around them, in the grass, more of the typical papers.

There were mass prayers books, group postcards showing the machine-gun unit standing in ranked and ruddy cheerfulness as in a football picture for a college annual; now they were humped and swollen in the grass; propaganda postcards showing a soldier in Austrian uniform bending a woman backward over a bed; the figures were impressionistically drawn; very attractively depicted and had nothing in common with actual rape in which the woman's skirts are pulled over her head to smother her, one comrade sometimes sitting upon

84

the head. There were many of these inciting cards which had evidently been issued just before the offensive. Now they were scattered with the smutty postcards, photographic; the small photographs of village girls by village photographers, the occasional pictures of children, and the letters, letters, letters. There was always much paper about the dead and the debris of this attack was no exception.

These were new dead and no one had bothered with anything but their pockets. Our own dead, or what he thought of, still, as our own dead, were surprisingly few, Nick noticed. Their coats had been opened too and their pockets were out, and they showed, by their positions, the manner and the skill of the attack. The hot weather had swollen them all alike regardless of nationality.

The town had evidently been defended, at the last, from the line of the sunken road and there had been few or no Austrians to fall back into it. There were only three bodies in the street and they looked to have been killed running. The houses of the town were broken by the shelling and the street had much rubble of plaster and mortar and there were broken beams, broken tiles, and many holes, some of them yellow-edged from the mustard gas. There were many pieces of shell, and shrapnel balls were scattered in the rubble. There was no one in the town at all.

Nick Adams had seen no one since he had left Fornaci, although, riding along the road through the over-foliaged country, he had seen guns hidden under screens of mulberry leaves to the left of the road, noticing them by the heat-waves in the air above the leaves where the sun hit the metal. Now he went on through the town, surprised to find it deserted, and came out on the low road beneath the bank of the river. Leaving the town there was a bare open space where the road slanted down and he could see the placid reach of the river and the low curve of the opposite bank and the whitened, sun-baked mud where the Austrians had dug. It was all very lush and overgreen since he had seen it last and becoming historical had made no change in this, the lower river.

The battalion was along the bank to the left. There was a series of holes in the top of the bank with a few men in them. Nick noticed where the machine-guns were posted and the signal rockets in their racks. The men in the holes in the side of the bank were sleeping. No one challenged. He went on and as he came around a turn in the mud bank a young second lieutenant with a stubble of beard and red-rimmed, very bloodshot eyes pointed a pistol at him.

'Who are you?'

Nick told him.

'How do I know this?'

Nick showed him the tessera with photograph and identification and the seal of the third army. He took hold of it.

'I will keep this.'

'You will not,' Nick said. 'Give me back the card and put your gun away. There, in the holster.'

'How am I to know who you are?'

'The tessera tells you.'

'And if the tessera is false? Give me that card.'

'Don't be a fool,' Nick said cheerfully. 'Take me to your company commander.'

'I should send you to battalion headquarters.'

'All right,' said Nick. 'Listen, do you know the Captain Paravicini? The tall one with the small moustache who was an architect and speaks English?'

'You know him?'

'A little.'

'What company does he command?'

'The second.'

'He is commanding the battalion.'

'Good,' said Nick. He was relieved to know that Para was all right. 'Let us go to the battalion.'

As Nick had left the edge of the town three shrapnel had burst high and to the right over one of the wrecked houses and since then there had been no shelling. But the face of this officer looked like the face of a man during a bombardment. There was the same tightness and the voice did not sound natural. His pistol made Nick nervous.

'Put it away,' he said. 'There's the whole river between them and you.'

'If I thought you were a spy I would shoot you now,' the second lieutenant said.

'Come on,' said Nick. 'Let us go to the battalion.' This officer made him very nervous.

The Captain Paravicini, acting major, thinner and more English-looking than ever, rose when Nick saluted from behind the table in the dugout that was battalion headquarters.

'Hello,' he said. 'I didn't know you. What are you doing in that uniform?'

'They've put me in it.'

'I am very glad to see you, Nicolo.'

'Right. You look well. How was the show?'

'We made a very fine attack. Truly. A very fine attack. I will show you. Look.'

He showed on the map how the attack had gone.

'I came from Fornaci,' Nick said. 'I could see how it had been. It was very good.'

'It was extraordinary. Altogether extraordinary. Are you attached to the regiment?'

'No. I am supposed to move around and let them see the uniform.'

'How odd.'

'If they see one American uniform that is supposed to make them believe others are coming.'

'But how will they know it is an American uniform?'

'You will tell them.'

'Oh. Yes, I see. I will send a corporal with you to show you about and you will make a tour of the lines.'

'Like a bloody politician,' Nick said.

'You would be much more distinguished in civilian clothes. They are what is really distinguished.'

'With a homburg hat,' said Nick.

'Or with a very furry fedora.'

'I'm supposed to have my pockets full of cigarettes and postal cards and such things,' Nick said. 'I should have a musette full of chocolate. These I should distribute with a kind word and a pat on the back. But there weren't any cigarettes and postcards and no chocolate. So they said to circulate around anyway.'

'I'm sure your appearance will be very heartening to the troops.'

'I wish you wouldn't,' Nick said. 'I feel badly enough about it as it is. In principle, I would have brought you a bottle of brandy.'

'In principle,' Para said and smiled, for the first time, showing yellowed teeth. 'Such a beautiful expression. Would you like some Grappa?'

'No, thank you,' Nick said.

'It hasn't any ether in it.'

'I can taste that still,' Nick remembered suddenly and completely.

'You know I never knew you were drunk until you started talking coming back in the camions.'

'I was stinking in every attack,' Nick said.

'I can't do it,' Para said. 'I took it in the first show, the very first show, and it only made me very upset and then frightfully thirsty.'

'You don't need it.'

'You're much braver in an attack than I am.'

'No,' Nick said. 'I know how I am and I prefer to get stinking. I'm not ashamed of it.'

'I've never seen you drunk.'

'No?' said Nick. 'Never? Not when we rode from Mestre to Portogrande that night and I wanted to go to sleep and used the bicycle for a blanket and pulled it up under my chin?'

'That wasn't in the lines.'

'Let's not talk about how I am,' Nick said. 'It's a subject I know too much about to want to think about it any more.'

'You might as well stay here a while,' Paravicini said. 'You can take a nap if you like. They didn't do much to this in the bombardment. It's too hot to go out yet.'

'I suppose there is no hurry.'

'How are you really?'

'I'm fine. I'm perfectly all right.'

'No. I mean really.'

'I'm all right. I can't sleep without a light of some sort. That's all I have now.'

'I said it should have been trepanned. I'm no doctor but I know that.'

'Well, they thought it was better to have it absorb, and that's what I got. What's the matter? I don't seem crazy to you, do I?'

'You seem in top-hole shape.'

'It's a hell of a nuisance once they've had you certified as nutty,' Nick said. 'No one ever has any confidence in you again.'

'I would take a nap, Nicolo,' Paravicini said. 'This isn't battalion headquarters as we used to know it. We're just waiting to be pulled out. You oughtn't to go out in the heat now – it's silly. Use that bunk.'

'I might just lie down,' Nick said.

Nick lay on the bunk. He was very disappointed that he felt this way and more disappointed, even, that it was so obvious to Captain Paravicini. This was not as large a dugout as the one where that platoon of the class of 1899, just out at the front, got hysterics during the bombardment before the attack, and Para had had him walk them two at a time outside to show them nothing would happen, he wearing his own chin strap tight across his mouth to keep his lips quiet. Knowing they could not hold it when they took it. Knowing it was all a bloody bells – If he can't stop crying, break his nose to give him something else to think about. I'd shoot one but it's too late now. They'd all be worse. Break his nose. They've put it back to five-twenty. We've only got four minutes more. Break that other silly bugger's nose and kick his silly ass out of here. Do you think they'll go over? If they don't, shoot two and try to scoop the others out some way. Keep behind them, sergeant. It's no use to walk ahead and find there's nothing coming behind you. Bail them out as you go. What a bloody bells. All right. That's right. Then, looking at the watch, in that quiet tone, that valuable quiet tone,

'Sovoia'. Making it cold, no time to get it, he couldn't find his own after the cave-in, one whole end had caved in; it was that started them; making it cold up that slope the only time he hadn't done it stinking. And after they came back the teleferica house burned, it seemed, and some of the wounded got down four days later and some did not get down, but we went up and we went back and we came down – we always came down. And there was Gaby Deslys, oddly enough, with feathers on; you called me baby doll a year ago tadada you said that I was rather nice to know tadada with feathers on, with feathers off, the great Gaby, and my name's Harry Pilcer, too, we used to step out of the far side of the taxis when it got steep going up the hill and he could see that hill every night when he dreamed with Sacré Cœur, blown white, like a soap bubble. Sometimes his girl was there and sometimes she was with someone else and he could not understand that, but those were the nights the river ran so much wider and stiller than it should and outside of Fossalta there was a low house painted yellow with willows all around it and a low stable and there was a canal, and he had been there a thousand times and never seen it, but there it was every night as plain as the hill, only it frightened him. That house meant more than anything and every night he had it. That was what he needed but it frightened him especially when the boat lay there quietly in the willows on the canal, but the banks weren't like this river. It was all lower, as it was in Portogrande, where they had seen them come wallowing across the flooded ground holding the rifles high until they fell with them in the water. Who ordered that one? If it didn't get so damned mixed up he could follow it all right. That was why he noticed everything in such detail to keep it all straight so he would know just where he was, but suddenly it confused without reason as now, he lying in a bunk at battalion headquarters, with Para commanding a battalion and he in a bloody American uniform. He sat up and looked around; they all watching him. Para was gone out. He lay down again.

The Paris part came earlier and he was not frightened of it except when she had gone off with someone else and the fear that they might take the same driver twice. That was what frightened about that. Never about the front. He never dreamed about the front now any more but what frightened him so that he could not get rid of it was that long yellow house and the different width of the river. Now he was back here at the river, he had gone through that same town, and there was no house. Nor was the river that way. Then where did he go each night; and what was the peril, and why would he wake, soaking wet, more frightened than he had ever been in a bombardment, because of a house and a long table and a canal?

He sat up, swung his legs carefully down; they stiffened any time they were out straight for long; returned the stares of the adjutant, the signallers and the two runners by the door and put on his cloth-covered trench helmet.

'I regret the absence of the chocolate, the postal cards and cigarettes,' he said. 'I am, however, wearing the uniform.'

'The Major is coming back at once,' the adjutant said. In that army an adjutant is not a commissioned officer.

'The uniform is not very correct,' Nick told them. 'But it gives you the idea. There will be several millions of Americans here shortly.'

'Do you think they will send Americans down here?' asked the adjutant.

'Oh, absolutely. Americans twice as large as myself, healthy, with clean hearts, sleep at night, never been wounded, never been blown up, never had their heads caved in, never been scared, don't drink, faithful to the girls they left behind them, many of them never had crabs, wonderful chaps. You'll see.'

'Are you an Italian?' asked the adjutant.

'No, American. Look at the uniform. Spagnolini made it but it's not quite correct.'

'A North or South American?'

'North,' said Nick. He felt it coming on now. He would quiet down.

'But you speak Italian.'

'Why not? Do you mind if I speak Italian? Haven't I a right to speak Italian?'

'You have Italian medals.'

'Just the ribbons and the papers. The medals come later. Or you give them to people to keep and the people go away; or they are lost with your baggage. You can purchase others in Milan. It is the papers that are of importance. You must not feel badly about them. You will have some yourself if you stay at the front long enough.'

'I am a veteran of the Iritrea campaign,' said the adjutant stiffly. 'I fought in Tripoli.'

'It's quite something to have met you,' Nick put out his hand. 'Those must have been trying days. I noticed the ribbons. Were you, by any chance, on the Carso?'

'I have just been called up for this war. My class was too old.'

'At one time I was under the age limit,' Nick said. 'But now I am reformed out of the war.'

'But why are you here now?'

'I am demonstrating the American uniform,' Nick said. 'Don't you think it is very significant? It is a little tight in the collar but you will see untold millions wearing this uniform swarming like locusts. The grasshopper, you know, what we call the grasshopper in America, is really a locust. The true grasshopper is small and green and comparatively feeble. You must not, however, make a confusion with the seven-year locust or cicada which emits a peculiar sustained sound which at the moment I cannot recall. I try to recall it but I cannot. I can almost hear it and then it is quite gone. You will pardon me if I break off our conversation?'

'See if you can find the major,' the adjutant said to one of the two runners. 'I can see you have been wounded,' he said to Nick.

'In various places,' Nick said. 'If you are interested in scars I can show you some very interesting ones but I would rather talk about grasshoppers. What we call grasshoppers that is; and what are, really, locusts. These insects at one time played a very important part in my life. It might interest you and you can look at the uniform while I am talking.'

The adjutant made a motion with his hand to the second runner who went out.

'Fix your eyes on the uniform. Spagnolini made it, you know. You might as well look, too,' Nick said to the signallers. 'I really have no rank. We're under the American consul. It's perfectly all right for you to look. You can stare, if you like. I will tell you about the American locust. We always preferred one that we called the medium-brown. They last the best in water and fish prefer them. The larger ones that fly make a noise somewhat similar to that produced by a rattlesnake rattling his rattlers, a very dry sound, have vivid coloured wings, some are bright red, others yellow barred with black, but their wings go to pieces in the winter and they make a very blowsy bait, while the medium-brown is a plump, compact, succulent hopper that I can recommend as far as one may well recommend something you gentlemen will probably never encounter. But I must insist that you will never gather a sufficient supply of these insects for a day's fishing by pursuing them with your hands or trying to hit them with a bat. That is sheer nonsense and a useless waste of time. I repeat, gentlemen, that you will get nowhere at it. The correct procedure, and one which should be taught all young officers at every small-arms course if I had anything to say about it, and who knows but what I will have, is the employment of a seine or net made of common mosquito netting. Two officers holding this length of netting at alternate ends, or let us say one at each end, stoop, hold the bottom extremity of the net in one hand and the top extremity in the other and run into the wind. The hoppers, flying with the wind, fly against the length of netting and are imprisoned in its folds. It is no trick at all to catch a very great quantity indeed, and no officer, in my opinion, should be without a length of mosquito netting suitable for the improvisation of one of these grasshopper seines. I hope I have made myself clear, gentlemen. Are there any questions? If there is anything in the course you do not understand please ask questions. Speak up. None? Then I would like to close on this note. In the words of that great soldier and gentleman, Sir Henry Wilson: Gentlemen, either you must govern or you must be governed. Let me repeat it. Gentlemen, there is one thing I would like to have you remember. One thing I would like you to take with you as you leave this room. Gentlemen, either you must govern – or you must be governed. That is all, gentlemen. Good day.'

He removed his cloth-covered helmet, put it on again and, stooping, went out the low entrance of the dugout. Para, accompanied by the two runners, was coming down the line of the sunken road. It was very hot in the sun and Nick removed the helmet.

'There ought to be a system for wetting these things,' he said. 'I shall wet this one in the river.' He started up the bank.

'Nicolo,' Paravicini called. 'Nicolo. Where are you going?'

'I don't really have to go,' Nick came down the slope, holding the helmet in his hands. 'They're a damned nuisance wet or dry. Do you wear yours all the time?'

'All the time,' said Para. 'It's making me bald. Come inside.' Inside Para told him to sit down.

'You know they're absolutely no damned good,' Nick said. 'I remember when they were a comfort when we first had them, but I've seen them full of brains too many times.'

'Nicolo,' Para said. 'I think you should go back. I think it would be better if you didn't come up to the line until you had those supplies. There's nothing here for you to do. If you move around, even with something worth giving away, the men will group and that invites shelling. I won't have it.'

'I know it's silly,' Nick said. 'It wasn't my idea. I heard the brigade was here so I thought I would see you or someone else I knew. I could have gone to Zenzon or to San Dona. I'd like to go to San Dona to see the bridge again.'

'I won't have you circulating around to no purpose,' Captain Paravicini said.

'All right,' said Nick. He felt it coming on again.

'You understand?'

'Of course,' said Nick. He was trying to hold it in.

'Anything of that sort should be done at night.'

'Naturally,' said Nick. He knew he could not stop it now.

'You see, I am commanding the battalion,' Para said.

'And why shouldn't you be?' Nick said. Here it came. 'You can read and write, can't you?'

'Yes,' said Para gently.

'The trouble is you have a damned small battalion to command. As soon as it gets to strength again they'll give you back your company. Why don't they bury the dead? I've seen them now. I don't care about seeing them again. They can bury them any time as far as I'm concerned and it would be much better for you. You'll all get bloody sick.'

'Where did you leave your bicycle?'

'Inside the last house.'

'Do you think it will be all right?'

'Don't worry,' Nick said. 'I'll go in a little while.'

'Lie down a little while, Nicolo.'

'All right.'

He shut his eyes and in place of the man with the beard who looked at him over the sights of the rifle, quite calmly before squeezing off, the white flash and clublike impact, on his knees, hot-sweet choking, coughing it on to the rock while they went past him, he saw a long, yellow house with a low stable and the river much wider than it was and stiller. 'Christ,' he said, 'I might as well go.'

He stood up.

'I'm going, Para,' he said. 'I'll ride back now in the afternoon. If any supplies have come I'll bring them down tonight. If not I'll come at night when I have something to bring.'

'It is still hot to ride,' Captain Paravicini said.

'You don't need to worry,' Nick said. 'I'm all right now for quite a while. I had one then but it was easy. They're getting much better. I can tell when I'm going to have one because I talk so much.'

'I'll send a runner with you.'

'I'd rather you didn't. I know the way.'

'You'll be back soon?'

'Absolutely.'

'Let me send –'

'No,' said Nick. 'As a mark of confidence.'

'Well, Ciaou then.'

'Ciaou,' said Nick. He started back along the sunken road toward where he had left the bicycle. In the afternoon the road would be shady once he had passed the canal. Beyond that there were trees on both sides that had not been shelled at all. It was on that stretch that, marching, they had once passed the Terza Savoia cavalry regiment riding in the snow with their lances. The horses' breath made plumes in the cold air. No, that was somewhere else. Where was that?

'I'd better get to that damned bicycle,' Nick said to himself. 'I don't want to lose the way to Fornaci.'

The Mother of a Queen

When his father died he was only a kid and his manager buried him perpetually. That is, so he would have the plot permanently. But when his mother died his manager thought they might not always be so hot on each other. They were sweethearts; sure he's a queen, didn't you know that, of course he is. So he just buried her for five years.

Well, when he came back to Mexico from Spain he got the first notice. It said it was the first notice that the five years were up and would he make arrangements for the continuing of his mothers' grave. It was only twenty dollars for perpetual. I had the cash box then and I said let me attend to it, Paco. But he said no, he would look after it. He'd look after it right away. It was his mother and he wanted to do it himself.

Then in a week he got the second notice. I read it to him and I said I thought he had looked after it.

No, he said, he hadn't.

'Let me do it,' I said. 'It's right here in the cash box.'

No, he said. Nobody could tell him what to do. He'd do it himself when he got around to it. 'What's the sense in spending money sooner than necessary?'

'All right,' I said, 'but see you look after it.' At this time he had a contract for six fights at four thousand pesos a fight besides his benefit fight. He made over fifteen thousand dollars there in the capital alone. He was just tight, that's all.

The third notice came in another week and I read it to him. It said that if he did not make the payment by the following Saturday his mother's gave would be opened and her remains dumped on the common boneheap. He said he would go attend to it that afternoon when he went to town.

'Why not have me do it?' I asked him.

'Keep out of my business,' he said. 'It's my business and I'm going to do it.'

'All right, if that's the way you feel about it,' I said. 'Do your own business.'

He got the money out of the cash box, although then he always carried a hundred or more pesos with him all the time, and he said he would look after it. He went out with the money and so of course I thought he had attended to it.

A week later the notice came that they had no response to the final warning and so his mother's body had been dumped on the boneheap; on the public boneheap.

'Jesus Christ,' I said to him, 'you said you'd pay that and you took money out of the cash box to do it and now what's happened to your mother? My God think of it! The public boneheap and your own mother. Why didn't you let me look after it? I would have sent it when the first notice came.'

'It's none of your business. It's *my* mother.'

'It's none of *my* business, yes, but it was *your* business. What kind of blood is it in a man that will let that be done to his mother? You don't deserve to have a mother.'

'It is my mother,' he said. 'Now she is so much dearer to me. Now I don't have to think of her buried in one place and be sad. Now she is all about me in the air, like the birds and the flowers. Now she will always be with me.'

'Jesus Christ,' I said, 'what kind of blood have you anyway? I don't want you even to speak to me.'

'She is all around me,' he said. 'Now I will never be sad.'

At that time he was spending all kinds of money around women trying to make himself seem a man and fool people, but it didn't have any effect on people that knew anything about him. He owed me over six hundred pesos and he wouldn't pay me. 'Why do you want it now?' he'd say. 'Don't you trust me? Aren't we friends?'

'It isn't friends or trusting you. It's that I paid the accounts out of my own money while you were away and now I need the money back and you have it to pay me.'

'I haven't got it.'

'You have it,' I said. 'It's in the cash box now and you can pay me.'

'I need that money for something,' he said. 'You don't know all the needs I have for money.'

'I stayed here all the time you were in Spain and you

authorized me to pay these things as they came up, all these things of the house, and you didn't send any money while you were gone and I paid over six hundred pesos in my own money and now I need it and you can pay me.'

'I'll pay you soon,' he said. 'Right now I need the money badly.'

'For what?'

'For my own business.'

'Why don't you pay me some on account?'

'I can't,' he said. 'I need that money too badly. But I will pay you.'

He had only fought twice in Spain, they couldn't stand him there, they saw through him quick enough, and he had seven new fighting suits made and this is the kind of thing he was: he had them packed so badly that four of them were ruined by sea water on the trip back and he couldn't even wear them.

'My God,' I said to him, 'you go to Spain. You stay there the whole season and only fight two times. You spend all the money you took with you on suits and then have them spoiled by salt water so you can't wear them. That is the kind of season you have and then you talk to me about running your own business. Why don't you pay me the money you owe me so I can leave?'

'I want you here,' he said, 'and I will pay you. But now I need the money.'

'You need it too badly to pay for your own mother's grave to keep your mother buried. Don't you?' I said.

'I am happy about what has happened to my mother,' he said. 'You cannot understand.'

'Thank Christ·I can't,' I said. 'You pay me what you owe me or I will take it out of the cash box.'

'I will keep the cash box myself,' he said.

'No, you won't,' I said.

That very afternoon he came to me with a punk, some fellow from his own town who was broke, and said, 'Here is a paesano who needs money to go home because his mother is very sick.' This fellow was just a punk, you understand, a nobody he'd never seen before, but from his home town, and he wanted to be the big, generous matador with a fellow townsman.

'Give him fifty pesos from the cash box,' he told me.

'You just told me you had no money to pay me,' I said. 'And now you want to give fifty pesos to this punk.'

'He is a fellow townsman,' he said, 'and he is in distress.'

'You bitch,' I said. I gave him the key of the cash box. 'Get it yourself. I'm going to town.'

'Don't be angry,' he said. 'I'm going to pay you.'

I got the car out to go to town. It was his car but he knew I drove it better than he did. Everything he did I could do better. He knew it. He couldn't even read and write. I was going to see somebody and see what I could do about making him pay me. He came out and said, 'I'm coming with you and I'm going to pay you. We are good friends. There is no need to quarrel.'

We drove into the city and I was driving. Just before we came into the town he pulled out twenty pesos.

'Here's the money,' he said.

'You motherless bitch,' I said to him and told him what he could do with the money. 'You give fifty pesos to that punk and then offer me twenty when you owe me six hundred. I wouldn't take a nickel from you. You know what you can do with it.'

I got out of the car without a peso in my pocket and I didn't know where I was going to sleep that night. Later I went out with a friend and got my things from his place. I never spoke to him again until this year. I met him walking with three friends in the evening on the way to the Callao cinema in the Gran Via in Madrid. He put his hand out to me.

'Hello, Roger, old friend,' he said to me. 'How are you? People say you are talking against me. That you say all sorts of unjust things about me.'

'All I say is you never had a mother,' I said to him. That's the worst thing you can say to insult a man in Spanish.

'That's true,' he said. 'My poor mother died when I was so young it seems as though I never had a mother. It's very sad.'

There's a queen for you. You can't touch them. Nothing,

nothing can touch them. They spend money on themselves or for vanity, but they never pay. Try to get one to pay. I told him what I thought of him right there on the Gran Via, in front of three friends, but he speaks to me now when I meet him as though we were friends. What kind of blood is it that makes a man like that?

One Reader Writes

She sat at the table in her bedroom with a newspaper folded open before her and only stopping to look out of the window at the snow which was falling and melting on the roofs as it fell. She wrote this letter, writing it steadily with no necessity to cross out or rewrite anything.

Roanoke, Virginia
6 February 1933

Dear Doctor,
   May I write you for some very important advice – I have a decision to make and don't know just whom to trust most, I dare not ask my parents – and so I come to you – and only because I need not see you, can I confide in you even. Now here is the situation – I married a man in U.S. service in 1929 and that same year he was sent to China, Shanghai – he stayed three years – and came home – he was discharged from the service some few months ago – and went to his mother's home, in Helena, Arkansas. He wrote for me to come home – I went, and found he is taking a course of injections and I naturally ask, and found he is being treated for I don't know how to spell the word but it sounds like this 'sifilus' – Do you know what I mean – now tell me will it ever be safe for me to live with him again – I did not come in close contact with him at any time since his return from China. He assures me he will be O.K. after this doctor finishes with him – Do you think it right – I often heard my Father say one could well wish themselves dead if once they became a victim of that malady – I believe my Father but want to believe my Husband most – Please, please tell me what to do – I have a daughter born while her Father was in China –
   Thanking you and trusting wholly in your advice
I am

and signed her name.

Maybe he can tell me what's right to do, she said to herself. Maybe he can tell me. In the picture in the paper he looks like he'd know. He looks smart, all right. Every day he tells somebody what to do. He ought to know. I want to do whatever is right. It's such a long time though. It's a long time. And it's been a long time. My Christ, it's been a long time. He had to go wherever they sent him, I know, but I don't know what he had to get it for. Oh, I wish to Christ he wouldn't have got it. I don't care what he did to get it. But I wish to Christ he hadn't ever got it. It does seem like he didn't have to have got it. I don't know what to do. I wish to Christ he hadn't got any kind of malady. I don't know why he had to get a malady.

Homage to Switzerland

Inside the station café it was warm and light. The wood of the tables shone from wiping and there were baskets of pretzels in glazed paper sacks. The chairs were carved, but the seats were worn and comfortable. There was a carved wooden clock on the wall and a bar at the far end of the room. Outside the window it was snowing.

Two of the station porters sat drinking new wine at the table under the clock. Another porter came in and said the Simplon-Orient Express was an hour late at Saint-Maurice. He went out. The waitress came over to Mr Wheeler's table.

'The Express is an hour late, sir,' she said. 'Can I bring you some coffee?'

'If you think it won't keep me awake.'

'Please?' asked the waitress.

'Bring me some,' said Mr Wheeler.

'Thank you.'

She brought the coffee from the kitchen and Mr Wheeler looked out the window at the snow falling in the light from the station platform.

'Do you speak other languages besides English?' he asked the waitress.

'Oh, yes, sir, I speak German and French and the dialects.'

'Would you like a drink or something?'

'Oh, no, sir. It is not permitted to drink in the café with the clients.'

'You won't take a cigar?'

'Oh, no, sir. I don't smoke, sir.'

'That is all right,' said Mr Wheeler. He looked out of the window again, drank the coffee, and lit a cigarette.

'Fräulein,' he called. The waitress came over.

'What would you like, sir?'

'You,' he said.

'You must not joke me like that.'

'I'm not joking.'

'Then you must not say it.'

'I haven't time to argue,' Mr Wheeler said. 'The train comes in forty minutes. If you'll go upstairs with me I'll give you a hundred francs.'

'You should not say such things, sir. I will ask the porter to speak with you.'

'I don't want a porter,' Mr Wheeler said. 'Nor a policeman, nor one of those boys that sell cigarettes. I want you.'

'If you talk like that you must go out. You cannot stay here and talk like that.'

'Why don't you go away then? If you go away I can't talk to you.'

The waitress went away. Mr Wheeler watched to see if she spoke to the porters. She did not.

'Mademoiselle!' he called. The waitress came over. 'Bring me a bottle of Sion, please.'

'Yes, sir.'

Mr Wheeler watched her go out, then come in with the wine and bring it to the table. He looked toward the clock.

'I'll give you two hundred francs,' he said.

'Please do not say such things.'

'Two hundred francs is a great deal of money.'

'You will not say such things!' the waitress said. She was losing her English. Mr Wheeler looked at her interestedly.

'Two hundred francs.'

'You are hateful.'

'Why don't you go away then? I can't talk to you if you're not here.'

The waitress left the table and went over to the bar. Mr Wheeler drank the wine and smiled to himself for some time.

'Mademoiselle,' he called. The waitress pretended not to hear him. 'Mademoiselle,' he called again. The waitress came over.

'You wish something?'

'Very much. I'll give you three hundred francs.'

'You are hateful.'

'Three hundred francs Swiss.'

She went away and Mr Wheeler looked after her. A porter opened the door. He was the one who had Mr Wheeler's bags in his charge.

'The train is coming, sir,' he said in French. Mr Wheeler stood up.

'Mademoiselle,' he called. The waitress came toward the table. 'How much is the wine?'

'Seven francs.'

Mr Wheeler counted out eight francs and left them on the table. He put on his coat and followed the porter on to the platform where the snow was falling.

'Au revoir, Mademoiselle,' he said. The waitress watched him go. He's ugly, she thought, ugly and hateful. Three hundred francs for a thing that is nothing to do. How many times have I done that for nothing. And no place to go here. If he had sense he would know there was no place. No time and no place to go. Three hundred francs to do that. What people those Americans.

Standing on the cement platform beside his bags, looking down the rails toward the headlight of the train coming through the snow, Mr Wheeler was thinking that it was very inexpensive sport. He had only spent, actually, aside from the dinner, seven francs for a bottle of wine and a franc for the tip. Seventy-five centimes would have been better. He would have felt better now if the tip had been seventy-five centimes. One franc Swiss is five francs French. Mr Wheeler was headed for Paris. He was very careful about money and did not care for women. He had been in that station before and he knew there was no upstairs to go to. Mr Wheeler never took chances.

PART II
MR JOHNSON TALKS ABOUT IT AT VEVEY

Inside the station café it was warm and light; the tables were shiny from wiping and on some there were red and white striped tablecloths; and there were blue and white striped tablecloths on others and on all of them baskets with pretzels in glazed paper sacks. The chairs were carved but the wood seats were worn and comfortable. There was a clock on the wall, a zinc bar at the far end of the room, and outside the window it was snowing. Two of the station porters sat drinking new wine at the table under the clock.

Another porter came in and said the Simplon-Orient Express was an hour late at Saint-Maurice. The waitress came over to Mr Johnson's table.

'The Express is an hour late, sir,' she said. 'Can I bring you some coffee?'

'If it's not too much trouble.'

'Please?' asked the waitress.

'I'll take some.'

'Thank you.'

She brought the coffee from the kitchen and Mr Johnson looked out the window at the snow falling in the light from the station platform.

'Do you speak other languages besides English?' he asked the waitress.

'Oh, yes, I speak German and French and the dialects.'

'Would you like a drink of something?'

'Oh, no, sir, it is not permitted to drink in the café with the clients.'

'Have a cigar?'

'Oh, no, sir,' she laughed. 'I don't smoke, sir.'

'Neither do I,' said Johnson. 'It's a dirty habit.'

The waitress went away and Johnson lit a cigarette and drank the coffee. The clock on the wall marked a quarter to ten. His watch was a little fast. The train was due at ten-thirty – an hour late meant eleven-thirty. Johnson called to the waitress.

'Signorina!'

'What would you like, sir?'

'You wouldn't like to play with me?' Johnson asked. The waitress blushed.

'No, sir.'

'I don't mean anything violent. You wouldn't like to make up a party to see the night life of Vevey? Bring a girl friend if you like.'

'I must work,' the waitress said. 'I have my duty here.'

'I know,' said Johnson. 'But couldn't you get a substitute? They used to do that in the Civil War.'

'Oh, no, sir. I must be here myself in person.'

'Where did you learn your English?'

'At the Berlitz school, sir.'

'Tell me about it,' Johnson said. 'Were the Berlitz undergraduates a wild lot? What about all this necking and petting? Were there many smoothies? Did you ever run into Scott Fitzgerald?'

'Please?'

'I mean were your college days the happiest days of your life? What sort of team did Berlitz have last fall?'

'You are joking, sir?'

'Only feebly,' said Johnson. 'You're an awfully good girl. And you don't want to play with me?'

'Oh, no, sir,' said the waitress. 'Would you like me to bring you something?'

'Yes,' said Johnson. 'Would you bring me the wine list?'

'Yes, sir.'

Johnson walked over with the wine list to the table where the three porters sat. They looked up at him. They were old men.

'Wollen Sie trinken?' he asked. One of them nodded and smiled.

'Oui, monsieur.'

'You speak French?'

'Oui, monsieur.'

'What shall we drink? Connais vous des champagnes?'

'Non, monsieur.'

'Faut les connaître,' said Johnson. 'Fräulein,' he called the waitress. 'We will drink champagne.'

'Which champagne would you prefer, sir?'

'The best,' said Johnson. 'Laquelle est le best?' he asked the porters.

'Le meilleur?' asked the porter who had spoken first.

'By all means.'

The porter took out a pair of gold-rimmed glasses from his coat pocket and looked over the list. He ran his finger down the four typewritten names and prices.

'Sportsman,' he said. 'Sportsman is the best.'

'You agree, gentlemen?' Johnson asked the other porters. The one porter nodded. The other said in French, 'I don't know them personally but I've often heard speak of Sportsman. It's good.'

'A bottle of Sportsman,' Johnson said to the waitress. He looked at the price on the wine card: eleven francs Swiss. 'Make it two Sportsmen. Do you mind if I sit here with you?' he asked the porter who had suggested Sportsman.

'Sit down. Put yourself here, please.' The porter smiled at him. He was folding his spectacles and putting them away in their case. 'Is it the gentleman's birthday?'

'No,' said Johnson. 'It's not a fête. My wife has decided to divorce me.'

'So,' said the porter. 'I hope not.' The other porter shook his head. The third porter seemed a little deaf.

'It is doubtless a common experience,' said Johnson, 'like the first visit to the dentist or the first time a girl is unwell, but I have been upset.'

'It is understandable,' said the oldest porter. 'I understand it.'

'None of you gentlemen is divorced?' Johnson asked. He had stopped clowning with the language and was speaking good French now and had been for some time.

'No,' said the porter who had ordered Sportsman. 'They don't divorce much here. There are gentlemen who are divorced but not many.'

'With us,' said Johnson, 'it's different. Practically everyone is divorced.'

'That's true,' the porter confirmed. 'I've read it in the paper.'

'I myself am somewhat in retard,' Johnson went on. 'This is the first time I have been divorced. I am thirty-five.'

'Mais vous êtes encore jeune,' said the porter. He explained to the two others. 'Monsieur n'a que trente-cinq ans.' The other porters nodded. 'He's very young,' said one.

'And it is really the first time you've been divorced?' asked the porter.

'Absolutely,' said Johnson. 'Please open the wine, mademoiselle.'

'And it is very expensive?'

'Ten thousand francs.'

'Swiss money?'

'No, French money.'

'Oh, yes. Two thousand francs Swiss. All the same it's not cheap.'

'No.'

'And why does one do it?'

'One is asked to.'

'But why do they ask that?'

'To marry someone else.'

'But it's idiotic.'

'I agree with you,' said Johnson. The waitress filled the four glasses. They all raised them.

'Prosit,' said Johnson.

'À votre santé, monsieur,' said the porter. The other two porters said 'Salut'. The champagne tasted like sweet pink cider.

'Is it a system always to respond in a different language in Switzerland?' Johnson asked.

'No,' said the porter. 'French is more cultivated. Besides, this is la Suisse Romande.'

'But you speak German?'

'Yes. Where I come from they speak German.'

'I see,' said Johnson, 'and you say you have never been divorced?'

'No. It would be too expensive. Besides, I have never married.'

'Ah,' said Johnson. 'And these other gentlemen?'

'They are married.'

'You like being married?' Johnson asked one of the porters.

'What?'

'You like the married state?'

'Oui. C'est normale.'

'Exactly,' said Johnson. 'Et vous, monsieur?'

'Ça va,' said the other porter.

'Pour moi,' said Johnson, 'ça ne va pas.'

'Monsieur is going to divorce,' the first porter explained.

'Oh,' said the second porter.

'Ah ha,' the third porter said.

'Well,' said Johnson, 'the subject seems to be exhausted. You're not interested in my troubles,' he addressed the first porter.

'But yes,' said the porter.

'Well, let's talk about something else.'

'As you wish.'

'What can we talk about?'

'You do the sport?'

'No,' said Johnson. 'My wife does, though.'

'What do you do for amusement?'

'I am a writer.'

'Does that make much money?'

'No. But later on when you get known it does.'

'It is interesting?'

'No,' said Johnson, 'it is not interesting. I am sorry, gentlemen, but I have to leave you. Will you please drink the other bottle?'

'But the train does not come for three-quarters of an hour.'

'I know,' said Johnson. The waitress came and he paid for the wine and his dinner.

'You going out, sir?' she asked.

'Yes,' said Johnson, 'just for a little walk. I'll leave my bag here.'

He put on his muffler, his coat, and his hat. Outside the snow was falling heavily. He looked back through the window at the three porters sitting at the table. The waitress was filling their glasses from the last wine of the opened bottle. She took the unopened bottle back to the bar. That makes them three francs something apiece, Johnson thought. He turned and walked down the platform. Inside the café he had thought that talking about it would blunt it; but it had not blunted it; it had made him feel nasty.

PART III
THE SON OF A FELLOW MEMBER AT TERRITET

In the station café at Territet it was a little too warm; the lights were bright and the tables shiny from polishing. There were baskets with pretzels in glazed paper sacks on the tables and cardboard pads for beer glasses in order that the moist glasses would not make rings on the wood. The chairs were carved but the wooden seats were worn and quite comfortable. There was a clock on the wall, a bar at the far end of the room, and outside the window it was snowing. There was an old man drinking coffee at a table under the clock and reading the evening paper. A porter came in and said the Simplon-Orient Express was an hour late at Saint-Maurice. The waitress came over to Mr Harris's table. Mr Harris had just finished dinner.

'The Express is an hour late, sir. Can I bring you some coffee?'

'If you like.'

'Please?' asked the waitress.

'All right,' said Mr Harris.

'Thank you, sir,' said the waitress.

She brought the coffee from the kitchen and Mr Harris put sugar in it, crunched the lumps with his spoon, and looked out of the window at the snow falling in the light from the station platform.

'Do you speak other languages besides English?' he asked the waitress.

'Oh, yes, sir. I speak German and French and the dialects.'

'Which do you like best?'

'They are all very much the same, sir. I can't say I like one better than another.'

'Would you like a drink of something or a coffee?'

'Oh, no, sir, it is not permitted to drink in the café with the clients.'

'You wouldn't take a cigar?'

'Oh, no, sir,' she laughed. 'I don't smoke, sir.'

'Neither do I,' said Harris. 'I don't agree with David Belasco.'

'Please?'

'Belasco. David Belasco. You can always tell him because he has his collar on backwards. But I don't agree with him. Then, too, he's dead now.'

'Will you excuse me, sir?' asked the waitress.

'Absolutely,' said Harris. He sat forward in the chair and looked out of the window. Across the room the old man had folded his paper. He looked at Mr Harris and then picked up his coffee cup and saucer and walked to Harris's table.

'I beg your pardon if I intrude,' he said in English, 'but it has just occurred to me that you might be a member of the National Geographic Society.'

'Please sit down,' Harris said. The gentleman sat down.

'Won't you have another coffee or a liqueur?'

'Thank you,' said the gentleman.

'Won't you have a kirsch with me?'

'Perhaps. But you must have it with me.'

'No, I insist.' Harris called the waitress. The old gentleman took out from an inside pocket of his coat a leather pocket-book. He took off a wide rubber band and drew out several papers, selected one, and handed it to Harris.

'That is my certificate of membership,' he said. 'Do you know Frederick J. Roussel in America?'

'I'm afraid I don't.'

'I believe he is very prominent.'

'Where does he come from? Do you know what part of the States?'

'From Washington, of course. Isn't that the headquarters of the Society?'

'I believe it is.'

'You believe it is. Aren't you sure?'

'I've been away a long time,' Harris said.

'You're not a member, then?'

'No. But my father is. He's been a member for a great many years.'

'Then he would know Frederick J. Roussel. He is one of the officers of the Society. You will observe that it is by Mr Roussel that I was nominated for membership.'

'I'm awfully glad.'

'I am sorry you are not a member. But you could obtain nomination through your father?'

'I think so,' said Harris. 'I must when I go back.'

'I would advise you to,' said the gentleman. 'You see the magazine, of course?'

'Absolutely.'

'Have you seen the number with the coloured plates of the North American fauna?'

'Yes. I have it in Paris.'

'And the number containing the panorama of the volcanoes of Alaska?'

'That was a wonder.'

'I enjoyed very much, too, the wild animal photographs of George Shiras three.'

'They were damned fine.'

'I beg your pardon?'

'They were excellent. That fellow Shiras –'

'You call him that fellow?'

'We're old friends,' said Harris.

'I see. You know George Shiras three. He must be very interesting.'

'He is. He's about the most interesting man I know.'

'And do you know George Shiras two? Is he interesting too?'

'Oh, he's not so interesting.'

'I should imagine he would be very interesting.'

'You know, a funny thing. He's not so interesting. I've often wondered why.'

'H'm,' said the gentleman. 'I should have thought anyone in that family would be interesting.'

'Do you remember the panorama of the Sahara Desert?' Harris asked.

'The Sahara Desert? That was nearly fifteen years ago.'

'That's right. That was one of my father's favourites.'

'He doesn't prefer the newer numbers?'

'He probably does. But he was very fond of the Sahara panorama.'

'It was excellent. But to me its artistic value far exceeded its scientific interest.'

'I don't know,' said Harris. 'The wind blowing all that sand and that Arab with his camel kneeling toward Mecca.'

'As I recall, the Arab was standing holding the camel.'

'You're quite right,' said Harris. 'I was thinking of Colonel Lawrence's book.'

'Lawrence's book deals with Arabia, I believe.'

'Absolutely,' said Harris. 'It was the Arab reminded me of it.'

'He must be a very interesting young man.'

'I believe he is.'

'Do you know what he is doing now?'

'He's in the Royal Air Force.'

'And why does he do that?'

'He likes it.'

'Do you know if he belongs to the National Geographic Society?'

'I wonder if he does.'

'He would make a very good member. He is the sort of person they want as a member. I would be very happy to nominate him if you think they would like to have him.'

'I think they would.'

'I have nominated a scientist from Vevey and a colleague of mine from Lauzanne and they were both elected. I believe they would be very pleased if I nominated Colonel Lawrence.'

'It's a splendid idea,' said Harris. 'Do you come here to the café often?'

'I come here for coffee after dinner.'

'Are you in the University?'

'I am not active any longer.'

'I'm just waiting for the train,' said Harris. 'I'm going up to Paris and sail from Havre for the States.'

'I have never been to America. But I would like to go very much. Perhaps I shall attend a meeting of the society some time. I would be very happy to meet your father.'

'I'm sure he would have liked to meet you but he died last year. Shot himself, oddly enough.'

'I am very truly sorry. I am sure his loss was a blow to science as well as to his family.'

'Science took it awfully well.'

'This is my card,' Harris said. 'His initials were E. J. instead of E. D. I know he would have liked to know you.'

'It would have been a great pleasure.' The gentleman took out a card from the pocket-book and gave it to Harris. It read:

DR SIGISMUND WYER, PH.D.
*Member of National Geographic
Society, Washington, D.C., U.S.A.*

'I will keep it very carefully, Harris said.

A Day's Wait

He came into the room to shut the windows while we were still in bed and I saw he looked ill. He was shivering, his face was white, and he walked slowly as though it ached to move.

'What's the matter, Schatz?'

'I've got a headache.'

'You better go back to bed.'

'No, I'm all right.'

'You go to bed. I'll see you when I'm dressed.'

But when I came downstairs he was dressed, sitting by the fire, looking a very sick and miserable boy of nine years. When I put my hand on his forehead I knew he had a fever.

'You go up to bed,' I said, 'you're sick.'

'I'm all right,' he said.

When the doctor came he took the boy's temperature.

'What is it?' I asked him.

'One hundred and two.'

Downstairs, the doctor left three different medicines in different coloured capsules with instructions for giving them. One was to bring down the fever, another a purgative, the third to overcome an acid condition. The germs of influenza can only exist in an acid condition, he explained. He seemed to know all about influenza and said there was nothing to worry about if the fever did not go above one hundred and four degrees. This was a light epidemic of flu and there was no danger if you avoided pneumonia.

Back in the room I wrote the boy's temperature down and made a note of the time to give the various capsules.

'Do you want me to read to you?'

'All right. If you want to,' said the boy. His face was very white and there were dark areas under his eyes. He lay still in the bed and seemed very detached from what was going on.

I read aloud from Howard Pyle's *Book of Pirates*; but I could see he was not following what I was reading.

'How do you feel, Schatz?' I asked him.

'Just the same, so far,' he said.

I sat at the foot of the bed and read to myself while I waited for it to be time to give another capsule. It would have been natural for him to go to sleep, but when I looked up he was looking at the foot of the bed, looking very strangely.

'Why don't you try to go to sleep? I'll wake you up for the medicine.'

'I'd rather stay awake.'

After a while he said to me, 'You don't have to stay in here with me, Papa, if it bothers you.'

'It doesn't bother me.'

'No, I mean you don't have to stay if it's going to bother you.'

I thought perhaps he was a little lightheaded and after giving him the prescribed capsules at eleven o'clock I went out for a while.

It was a bright, cold day, the ground covered with a sleet that had frozen so that it seemed as if all the bare trees, the bushes, the cut brush and all the grass and the bare ground had been varnished with ice. I took the young Irish setter for a little walk up the road and along a frozen creek, but it was difficult to stand or walk on the glassy surface and the red dog slipped and slithered and I fell twice, hard, once dropping my gun and having it slide away over the ice.

We flushed a covey of quail under a high bank with overhanging brush and I killed two as they went out of sight over the top of the bank. Some of the covey lit in trees, but most of them scattered into brush piles and it was necessary to jump on the ice-coated mounds of brush several times before they would flush. Coming out while you were poised unsteadily on the icy, springy brush they made difficult shooting and I killed two, missed five, and started back pleased to have found a covey close to the house and happy there were so many left to find on another day.

At the house they said the boy had refused to let anyone come into the room.

'You can't come in,' he said. 'You mustn't get what I have.'

I went up to him and found him in exactly the position I

had left him, white-faced, but with the tops of his cheeks flushed by the fever, staring still, as he had stared, at the foot of the bed.

I took his temperature.

'What is it?'

'Something like a hundred,' I said. It was one hundred and two and four-tenths.

'It was a hundred and two,' he said.

'Who said so?'

'The doctor.'

'Your temperature is all right,' I said. 'It's nothing to worry about.'

'I don't worry,' he said, 'but I can't keep from thinking.'

'Don't think,' I said. 'Just take it easy.'

'I'm taking it easy,' he said, and looked straight ahead. He was evidently holding tight on to himself about something.

'Take this with water.'

'Do you think it will do any good?'

'Of course it will.'

I sat down and opened the *Pirate* book and commenced to read, but I could see he was not following, so I stopped.

'About what time do you think I'm going to die?' he asked.

'What?'

'About how long will it be before I die?'

'You aren't going to die. What's the matter with you?'

'Oh, yes, I am. I heard him say a hundred and two.'

'People don't die with a fever of one hundred and two. That's a silly way to talk.'

'I know they do. At school in France the boys told me you can't live with forty-four degrees. I've got a hundred and two.'

He had been waiting to die all day, ever since nine o'clock in the morning.

'You poor Schatz,' I said. 'Poor old Schatz. It's like miles and kilometres. You aren't going to die. That's a different thermometer. On that thermometer thirty-seven is normal. On this kind it's ninety-eight.

'Absolutely,' I said. 'It's like miles and kilometres. You

know, like how many kilometres we make when we do seventy miles in the car?'

'Oh,' he said.

But his gaze at the foot of the bed relaxed slowly. The hold over himself relaxed too, finally, and the next day it was very slack and he cried very easily at little things that were of no importance.

A Natural History of the Dead

It has always seemed to me that the war has been omitted as a field for the observations of the naturalist. We have charming and sound accounts of the flora and fauna of Patagonia by the late W. H. Hudson, the Reverend Gilbert White has written most interestingly of the Hoopoe on its occasional and not at all common visits to Selborne, and Bishop Stanley has given us a valuable, although popular, *Familiar History of Birds*. Can we not hope to furnish the reader with a few rational and interesting facts about the dead? I hope so.

When that persevering traveller, Mungo Park, was at one period of his course fainting in the vast wilderness of an African desert, naked and alone, considering his days as numbered and nothing appearing to remain for him to do but to lie down and die, a small moss-flower of extraordinary beauty caught his eye. 'Though the whole plant,' says he, 'was no larger than one of my fingers, I could not contemplate the delicate formation of its roots, leaves and capsules without admiration. Can that Being who planted, watered and brought to perfection, in this obscure part of the world, a thing which appears of so small importance, look with unconcern upon the situation and suffering of creatures formed after his own image? Surely not. Reflections like these would not allow me to despair; I started up and, disregarding both hunger and fatigue, travelled forward, assured that relief was at hand: and I was not disappointed.'

With a disposition to wonder and adore in like manner, as Bishop Stanley says, can any branch of Natural History be studied without increasing that faith, love and hope which we also, every one of us, need in our journey through the wilderness of life? Let us therefore see what inspiration we may derive from the dead.

In war the dead are usually the male of the human species, although this does not hold true with animals, and I have frequently seen dead mares among the horses. An interesting aspect of war, too, is that it is only there that the naturalist has an opportunity to observe the dead of mules. In twenty years of observation in civil life I had never seen a dead mule and had begun to entertain doubts as to whether these animals were really mortal. On rare occasions I had seen what I took to be dead mules, but on close approach these always proved to be living creatures who seemed to be dead through their quality of complete repose. But in war these animals succumb in much the same manner as the more common and less hardy horse.

Most of the mules that I saw dead were along mountain roads or lying at the foot of steep declivities whence they had been pushed to rid the road of their encumbrance. They seemed a fitting enough sight in the mountains where one was accustomed to their presence, and looked less incongruous there than they did later, at Smyrna, where the Greeks broke the legs of all their baggage animals and pushed them off the quay into the shallow water to drown. The numbers of broken-legged mules and horses drowning in the shallow water called for a Goya to depict them. Although, speaking literally, one can hardly say that they called for a Goya since there has only been one Goya, long dead, and it is extremely doubtful if these animals, were they able to call, would call for pictorial representation of their plight but, more likely, would, if they were articulate, call for someone to alleviate their condition.

Regarding the sex of the dead it is a fact that one becomes so accustomed to the sight of all the dead being men that the sight of a dead woman is quite shocking. I first saw inversion of the usual sex of the dead after the explosion of a munition factory which had been situated in the countryside near Milan, Italy. We drove to the scene of the disaster in trucks along poplar-shaded roads, bordered with ditches containing much minute animal life, which I could not clearly observe because of the great clouds of dust raised by the trucks. Arriving where the munition plant had been, some of us were put to patrolling about those large stocks of munitions which for some reason had not exploded, while others were put at extinguishing a fire which had gotten into the grass of an adjacent field; which task being concluded, we were ordered to search the immediate vicinity and surrounding fields for bodies. We found and carried to an improvised mortuary a good number of these and, I must admit, frankly, the shock it was to find that these dead were women rather than men. In those days women had not yet commenced to wear their hair cut short, as they did later for several years in Europe and America, and the most disturbing thing, perhaps because it was the most unaccustomed, was the presence, and, even more disturbing, the occasional absence of this long hair. I remember that after we had searched quite thoroughly for the complete dead we collected fragments. Many of these were detached from a heavy, barbed-wire fence which had surrounded the position of the factory and from the still existent portions of which we picked many of these detached bits which illustrated only too well the tremendous energy of high explosive. Many fragments we found a considerable distance away in the fields, they being carried farther by their own weight.

On our return to Milan I recall one or two of us discussing the occurrence and agreeing that the quality of unreality and the fact that there were no wounded did much to rob the disaster of a horror which might have been much greater. Also the fact that it had been so immediate and that the dead were in consequence still as little unpleasant as possible to carry and deal with made it quite removed from the usual battlefield experience. The pleasant, though dusty, ride through the beautiful Lombard countryside also was a compensation for the unpleasantness of the duty and on our return, while we exchanged impressions, we all agreed that it was indeed fortunate that the fire which broke out just before we arrived had been brought under control as rapidly as it had and before it had attained any of the seemingly huge stocks of unexploded munitions. We agreed too that the picking up of the fragments had been an extraordinary business; it being amazing that the human body should be blown into pieces which exploded along no anatomical lines, but rather divided as capriciously as the fragmentation in the burst of a high explosive shell.

A naturalist, to obtain accuracy of observation, may confine himself in his observations to one limited period and I will take first that following the Austrian offensive of June 1918 in Italy as one in which the dead were present in their greatest numbers, a withdrawal having been forced and an advance later made to recover the ground lost so that the positions after the battle were the same as before except for the presence of the dead. Until the dead are buried they change somewhat in appearance each day. The colour change in Caucasian races is from white to yellow, to yellow-green, to black. If left long enough in the heat the flesh comes to resemble coal-tar, especially where it has been broken or torn, and it has quite a visible tar-like iridescence. The dead grow larger each day until sometimes they become quite too big for their uniforms, filling these until they seem blown tight enough to burst. The individual members may increase in girth to an unbelievable extent and faces fill as taut and globular as balloons. The surprising thing, next to their progressive corpulence, is the amount of paper that is scattered about the dead. Their ultimate position, before there is any question of burial, depends on the location of the pockets in the uniform. In the Austrian army these pockets were in the back of the breeches and the dead, after a short time, all consequently lay on their faces, the two hip pockets pulled out and, scattered around them in the grass, all those papers their pockets contained. The heat, the flies, the indicative positions of the bodies in the grass, and the amount of paper scattered are the impressions one retains. The smell of battlefield in hot weather one cannot recall. You can remember that there was such a smell, but nothing ever happens to you to bring it back. It is unlike the smell of a regiment, which may come to you suddenly while riding in the street car and you will look across and see the man who has brought it to you. But the other thing is gone as completely as when you have been in love; you remember things that happened, but the sensation cannot be recalled.

One wonders what that persevering traveller, Mungo Park,

would have seen on a battlefield in hot weather to restore his confidence. There were always poppies in the wheat in the end of June, and in July, and the mulberry trees were in full leaf and one could see the heat waves rise from the barrels of the guns where the sun struck them through the screens of leaves; the earth was turned a bright yellow at the edge of holes where mustard gas shells had been and the average broken house is finer to see than one that has been shelled, but few travellers would take a good full breath of that early summer air and have any such thoughts as Mungo Park about those formed in His own image.

The first thing that you found about the dead was that, hit badly enough, they died like animals. Some quickly from a little wound you would not think would kill a rabbit. They died from little wounds as rabbits die sometimes from three or four small grains of shot that hardly seem to break the skin. Others would die like cats; a skull broken in and iron in the brain, they lie alive two days like cats that crawl into the coal bin with a bullet in the brain and will not die until you cut their heads off. Maybe cats do not die then, they say they have nine lives. I do not know, but most men die like animals, not men. I'd never seen a natural death, so called, and so I blamed it on the war and like the persevering traveller, Mungo Park, knew that here was something else, that always absent something else, and then I saw one.

The only natural death I've ever seen, outside of loss of blood, which isn't bad, was death from Spanish influenza. In this you drown in mucus, choking and how you know the patient's dead is: at the end he turns to be a little child again, though with his manly force, and fills the sheets as full as any diaper with one vast, final, yellow cataract that flows and dribbles on after he's gone. So now I want to see the death of any self-called Humanist* because a persevering traveller like Mungo Park or me lives on and maybe yet will live to see the

---

* The Reader's indulgence is requested for this mention of an extinct phenomenon. The reference, like all references to fashions, dates the story, but it is retained because of its mild historical interest and because its omission would spoil the rhythm.

actual death of members of this literary sect and watch the noble exits that they make. In my musings as a naturalist it has occurred to me that while decorum is an excellent thing some must be indecorous if the race is to be carried on since the position prescribed for procreation is indecorous, highly indecorous, and it occured to me that perhaps that is what these people are, or were: the children of decorous cohabitation. But regardless of how they started I hope to see the finish of a few, and speculate how worms will try that long preserved sterility; with their quaint pamphlets gone to bust and into footnotes all their lust.

While it is, perhaps, legitimate to deal with these self-designated citizens in a natural history of the dead, even though the designation may mean nothing by the time this work is published, yet it is unfair to the other dead, who were not dead in their youth of choice, who owned no magazines, many of whom had doubtless never even read a review, that one has seen in the hot weather with a half-pint of maggots working where their mouths have been. It was not always hot weather for the dead, much of the time it was the rain that washed them clean when they lay in it and made the earth soft when they were buried in it and sometimes then kept on until the earth was mud and washed them out and you had to bury them again. Or in the winter in the mountains you had to put them in the snow and when the snow melted in the spring someone else had to bury them. They had beautiful burying grounds in the mountains, war in the mountains is the most beautiful of all war, and in one of them, at a place called Pocol, they buried a general who was shot through the head by a sniper. This is where those writers are mistaken who write books called *Generals Die in Bed*, because this general died in a trench dug in snow, high in the mountains, wearing an Alpini hat with an eagle father in it and a hole in front you couldn't put your little finger in and a hole in back you could put your fist in, if it were a small fist and you wanted to put it there, and much blood in the snow. He was a damned fine general, and so was General von Behr who commanded the Bavarian Alpenkorps troops at the battle of Caporetto and was killed in his staff car by the Italian rearguard as he drove into Udine ahead of his troops, and the titles of all such books should be *Generals Usually Die in Bed*, if we are to have any sort of accuracy in such things.

In the mountains, too, sometimes, the snow fell on the dead outside the dressing station on the side that was protected by the mountain from any shelling. They carried them into a cave that had been dug into the mountainside before the earth froze. It was in this cave that a man whose head was broken as a flower-pot may be broken, although it was all held together by membranes and a skilfully applied bandage now soaked and hardened, with the structure of his brain disturbed by a piece of broken steel in it, lay a day, a night, and a day. The stretcher-bearers asked the doctor to go in and have a look at him. They saw him each time they made a trip and even when they did not look at him they heard him breathing. The doctor's eyes were red and the lids swollen, almost shut from tear gas. He looked at the man twice; once in daylight, once with a flashlight. That too would have made a good etching for Goya, the visit with the flashlight, I mean. After looking at him the second time the doctor believed the stretcher-bearers when they said the soldier was still alive.

'What do you want me to do about it?' he asked.

There was nothing they wanted done. But after a while they asked permission to carry him out and lay him with the badly wounded.

'No. No. No!' said the doctor, who was busy. 'What's the matter? Are you afraid of him?'

'We don't like to hear him in there with the dead.'

'Don't listen to him. If you take him out there you will have to carry him right back in.'

'We wouldn't mind that, Captain Doctor.'

'No,' said the Doctor. 'No. Didn't you hear me say no?'

'Why don't you give him an overdose of morphine?' asked an artillery officer who was waiting to have a wound in his arm dressed.

'Do you think that is the only use I have for morphine? Would you like me to have to operate without morphine? You have a pistol, go out and shoot him yourself.'

'He's been shot already,' said the officer. 'If some of you doctors were shot you'd be different.'

'Thank you very much,' said the doctor, waving a forceps in the air. 'Thank you a thousand times. What about these eyes?' He pointed the forceps at them. 'How would you like these?'

'Tear gas. We call it lucky if it's tear gas.'

'Because you leave the line,' said the doctor. 'Because you come running here with your tear gas to be evacuated. You rub onions in your eyes.'

'You are beside yourself. I do not notice your insults. You are crazy.'

The stretcher-bearers came in.

'Captain Doctor,' one of them said.

'Get out of here!' said the doctor.

They went out.

'I will shoot the poor fellow,' the artillery officer said. 'I am a humane man. I will not let him suffer.'

'Shoot him then,' said the doctor. 'Shoot him. Assume the responsibility. I will make a report. Wounded shot by lieutenant of artillery in first curing post. Shoot him. Go ahead, shoot him.'

'You are not a human being.'

'My business is to care for the wounded, not to kill them. That is for gentlemen of the artillery.'

'Why don't you care for him then?'

'I have done so. I have done all that can be done.'

'Why don't you send him down on the cable railway?'

'Who are you to ask me questions? Are you my superior officer? Are you in command of this dressing-post? Do me the courtesy to answer.'

The lieutenant of artillery said nothing. The others in the room were all soldiers and there were no other officers present.

'Answer me,' said the doctor, holding a needle up in his forceps. 'Give me a response.'

'F— yourself,' said the artillery officer.

'So,' said the doctor. 'So, you said that. All right. All right. We shall see.'

The lieutenant of artillery stood up and walked toward him.

'F— yourself,' he said. 'F— yourself. F— your mother. F— your sister . . .'

The doctor tossed the saucer full of iodine in his face. As he came toward him, blinded, the lieutenant fumbled for his pistol. The doctor skipped quickly behind him, tripped him and, as he fell to the floor, kicked him several times and picked up the pistol in his rubber gloves. The lieutenant sat on the floor holding his good hand to his eyes.

'I'll kill you!' he said. 'I'll kill you as soon as I can see.'

'I am the boss,' said the doctor. 'All is forgiven since you know I am the boss. You cannot kill me because I have your pistol. Sergeant! Adjutant! Adjutant!'

'The adjutant is at the cable railway,' said the sergeant.

'Wipe out this officer's eyes with alcohol and water. He has got iodine in them. Bring me the basin to wash my hands. I will take this officer next.'

'You won't touch me.'

'Hold him tight. He is a little delirious.'

One of the stretcher-bearers came in.

'Captain Doctor.'

'What do you want?'

'The man in the dead-house —'

'Get out of here.'

'Is dead, Captain Doctor. I thought you would be glad to know.'

'See, my poor lieutenant? We dispute about nothing. In time of war we dispute about nothing.'

'F— you,' said the lieutenant of artillery. He still could not see. 'You've blinded me.'

'It is nothing,' said the doctor. 'Your eyes will be all right. It is nothing. A dispute about nothing.'

'Ayee! Ayee! Ayee!' suddenly screamed the lieutenant. 'You have blinded me! You have blinded me!'

'Hold him tight,' said the doctor. 'He is in much pain. Hold him very tight.'

Wine of Wyoming

It was a hot afternoon in Wyoming; the mountains were a long way away and you could see snow on their tops, but they made no shadow, and in the valley the grain-fields were yellow, the road was dusty with cars passing, and all the small wooden houses at the edge of town were baking in the sun. There was a tree made shade over Fontan's back porch and I sat there at a table and Madame Fontan brought up cold beer from the cellar. A motor car turned off the main road and came up the side road, and stopped beside the house. Two men got out and came in through the gate. I put the bottles under the table. Madame Fontan stood up.

'Where's Sam?' one of the men asked at the screen door.

'He ain't here. He's at the mines.'

'You got some beer?'

'No. Ain't got any beer. That's a last bottle. All gone.'

'What's he drinking?'

'That's a last bottle. All gone.'

'Go on, give us some beer. You know me.'

'Ain't got any beer. That's a last bottle. All gone.'

'Come on, let's go some place where we can get some real beer,' one of them said, and they went out to the car. One of them walked unsteadily. The motor car jerked in starting, whirled on the road, and went on and away.

'Put the beer on the table,' Madame Fontan said. 'What's the matter, yes, all right. What's the matter? Don't drink off the floor.'

'I don't know who they were,' I said.

'They're drunk,' she said. 'That's what makes the trouble. Then they go somewhere else and say they got it here. Maybe they don't even remember.' She spoke French, but it was only French occasionally, and there were many English words and some English constructions.

'Where's Fontan?'

'Il fait de la vendange. Oh, my God, il est crazy pour le vin.'

'But you like the beer?'

'Oui, j'aime la bière, mais Fontan, il est crazy pour le vin.'

She was a plump old woman with a lovely ruddy complexion and white hair. She was very clean and the house was very clean and neat. She came from Lens.

'Where did you eat?'

'At the hotel.'

'Mangez ici. Il ne faut pas manger à l'hôtel ou au restaurant. Mangez ici!'

'I don't want to make you trouble. And besides they eat all right at the hotel.'

'I never eat at the hotel. Maybe they eat all right there. Only once in my life I ate at a restaurant in America. You know what they gave me? They gave me pork that was raw!'

'Really?'

'I don't lie to you. It was pork that wasn't cooked! Et mon fils il est marié avec une américaine, et tout le temps il a mangé les *beans* en *can*.'

'How long has he been married?'

'Oh, my God, I don't know. His wife weighs two hundred twenty-five pounds. She don't work. She don't cook. She gives him beans en can.'

'What does she do?'

'All the time she reads. Rien que des books. Tout le temps elle stay in bed and read books. Already she can't have another baby. She's too fat. There ain't any room.'

'What the matter with her?'

'She reads books all the time. He's a good boy. He works hard. He worked in the mines, now he works on a ranch. He never worked on a ranch before, and the man that owns the ranch said to Fontan that he never saw anybody work better on that ranch than that boy. Then he comes home and she feeds him nothing.'

'Why doesn't he get a divorce?'

'He ain't got no money to get a divorce. Besides, il est *crazy* pour elle.'

'Is she beautiful?'

'He thinks *so*. When he brought her home I thought I

would die. He's such a good boy and works hard all the time and never run around or make any trouble. Then he goes away to work in the oilfields and brings home this Indienne that weighs right then one hundred eighty-five pounds.'

'Elle est Indienne?'

'She's Indian all right. My God, yes. All the time she says sonofa bitsh goddam. She don't work.'

'Where is she now?'

'Au show.'

'Where's that?'

'*Au show. Moving* pictures. All she does is read and go to the show.'

'Have you got any more beer?'

'My God, yes. Sure. You come and eat with us tonight.'

'All right. What should I·bring.'

'Don't bring anything. Nothing at all. Maybe Fontan will have some of the wine.'

That night I had dinner at Fontan's. We ate in the dining-room and there was a clean tablecloth. We tried the new wine. It was very light and clear and good, and still tasted of the grapes. At the table there were Fontan and Madame and the little boy, André.

'What did you do today?' Fontan asked. He was an old man with small mine-tired body, a drooping grey moustache, and bright eyes, and was from the Centre near Saint-Étienne.

'I worked on my book.'

'Were your books all right?' asked Madame.

'He means he writes a book like a writer. Un roman,' Fontan explained.

'Pa, can I go to the show?' André asked.

'Sure,' said Fontan. André turned to me.

'How old do you think I am? Do you think I look fourteen years old?' He was a thin little boy, but his face looked sixteen.

'Yes. You look fourteen.'

'When I go to the show I crouch down like this and try to look small.' His voice was very high and breaking. 'If I give them a quarter they keep it all, but if I give them only fifteen cents they let me in all right.'

'I only give you fifteen cents, then,' said Fontan.

'No. Give me the whole quarter. I'll get it changed on the way.'

'Il faut revenir tout de suite après le show,' Madame Fontan said.

'I come right back.' André went out the door. The night was cooling outside. He left the door open and a cool breeze came in.

'Mangez!' said Madame Fontan. 'You haven't eaten anything.' I had eaten two helpings of chicken and French fried potatoes, three ears of sweet corn, some sliced cucumbers, and two helpings of salad.

'Perhaps he wants some kek,' Fontan said.

'I should have gotten some kek for him,' Madame Fontan said. 'Mangez du fromage. Mangez du crimcheez. Vous n'avez rien mangé. I ought have gotten kek. Americans always eat kek.'

'Mais j'ai rudement bien mangé.'

'Mangez! Vous n'avez rien mangé. Eat it all. We don't save anything. Eat it all up.'

'Eat some more salad,' Fontan said.

'I'll get some more beer,' Madame Fontan said. 'If you work all day in a book-factory you get hungry.'

'Elle ne comprend pas que vous êtes écrivain,' Fontan said. He was a delicate old man who used the slang and knew the popular songs of his period of military service in the end of the 1890s. 'He writes the books himself,' he explained to Madame.

'You write the books yourself?' Madame asked.

'Sometimes.'

'Oh!' she said. 'Oh! You write them yourself. Oh! Well, you get hungry if you do that too. Mangez! Je vais chercher de la bière.'

We heard her walking on the stairs to the cellar. Fontan smiled at me. He was very tolerant of people who had not his experience and wordly knowledge.

When André came home from the show we were still sitting in the kitchen and were talking about hunting.

'Labour *day* we all went to Clear Creek,' Madamé said. 'Oh, my God, you ought to have been there all right. We all went in the truck. Tout le monde est allé dans le truck. Nous sommes partis le dimanche. C'est le truck de Charley.'

'On a mangé, on a bu du vin, de la bière, et il y avait aussi un français qui a apporté de l'absinthe,' Fontan said. 'Un français de la Californie!'

'My God, nous avons chanté. There's a farmer comes to see what's the matter, and we give him something to drink, and he stayed with us awhile. There was some Italians come too, and they want to stay with us too. We sung a song about the Italians and they don't understand it. They didn't know we didn't want them, but we didn't have nothing to do with them, and after a while they went away.'

'How many fish did you catch?'

'Très peu. We went to fish a little while, but then we came back to sing again. Nous avons chanté, vous savez.'

'In the night,' said Madame, 'toutes les femmes dort dans le truck. Les hommes à côté du feu. In the night I hear Fontan come to get some more wine, and I tell him, Fontan, my God, leave some for tomorrow. Tomorrow they won't have anything to drink, and then they'll be sorry.'

'Mais nous avons tout bu,' Fontan said. 'Et le lendemain il ne reste rien.'

'What did you do?'

'Nous avons pêché sérieusement.'

'Good trout, all right, too. My God, yes. All the same; half-pound one ounce.'

'How big?'

'Half-pound one ounce. Just right to eat. All the same size; half-pound one ounce.'

'How do you like America?' Fontan asked me.

'It's my country, you see. So I like it, because it's my country. Mais on ne mange pas très bien. D'antan, oui. Mais maintenant, no.'

'No,' said Madame. 'On ne mange pas bien.' She shook her

head. 'Et aussi, il y a trop de Polack. Quand j'étais petite ma mère m'a dit, "vous mangez comme les Polacks." Je n'ai jamais compris ce que c'est qu'un Polack. Mais maintenant en Amérique je comprends. Il y a trop de Polack. Et, my God, ils sont sales, les Polacks.'

'It is fine for hunting and fishing,' I said.

'Oui. Ça, c'est le meilleur. La chasse et la pêche,' Fontan said. 'Qu'est-ce que vous avec comme fusil?'

'A twelve-gauge pump.'

'Il est bon, le pump,' Fontan nodded his head.

'Je veux aller à la chasse moi-même,' André said in his high little boy's voice.

'Tu ne peux pas,' Fontan said. He turned to me.

'Ils sont des sauvages, les boys, vous savez. Ils sont des sauvages. Ils veulent shooter les uns les autres.'

'Je veux aller tout seul,' André said, very shrill and excited.

'You can't go,' Madame Fontan said. 'You are too young.'

'Je veux aller tout seul,' André said shrilly. 'Je veux shooter les rats d'eau.'

'What are rats d'eau?' I asked.

'You don't know them? Sure you know them. What they call the muskrats.'

André had brought the twenty-two-calibre rifle out from the cupboard and was holding it in his hands under the light.

'Ils sont des sauvages,' Fontan explained. 'Ils veulent shooter les uns les autres.'

'Je veux aller tout seul,' André shrilled. He looked desperately along the barrel of the gun. 'Je vous shooter les rats d'eau. Je connais beaucoup de rats d'eau.'

'Give me the gun,' Fontan said. He explained again to me. 'They're savages. They would shoot one another.'

André held tight on to the gun.

'On peut looker. On ne fait pas de mal. On peut looker.'

'Il est crazy pour le shooting,' Madame Fontan said. 'Mais il est trop jeune.'

André put the twenty-two-calibre rifle back in the cupboard.

'When I'm bigger I'll shoot the muskrats and the jackrabbits, too,' he said in English. 'One time I went out with papa and he shot a jack-rabbit just a little bit and I shot it and hit it.'

'C'est vrai,' Fontan nodded. 'Il a tué un jack.'

'But he hit it first,' André said. 'I want to go all by myself and shoot all by myself. Next year I can do it.' He went over in a corner and sat down to read a book. I had picked it up when we came into the kitchen to sit after supper. It was a library book – *Frank on a Gunboat*.

'Il aime les books,' Madame Fontan said. 'But it's better than to run around at night with the older boys and steal things.'

'Books are all right,' Fontan said. 'Monsieur il fait les books.'

'Yes, that's so, all right. But too many books are bad,' Madame Fontan said. 'Ici, c'est une maladie, les books. C'est comme les churches. Ici il y a trop de churches. En France il y a seulement les catholiques et les protestants – et très peu de protestants. Mais ici rien que de churches. Quand j'étais venu ici je disais, oh, my God, what are all the churches?'

'C'est vrai,' Fontan said. 'Il y a trop de churches.'

'The other day,' Madame Fontan said, 'there was a little French girl here with her mother, the cousin of Fontan, and she said to me, "En Amérique il ne faut pas être catholique. It's not good to be catholique. The Americans don't like you to be catholique. It's like the dry law." I said to her, "What are you going to be? Heh? It's better to be catholique if you're catholique." But she said, "No, it isn't any good to be catholique in America." But I think it's better to be catholique if you are. Ce n'est pas bon de changer sa religion. My God, no.'

'You go to the mass here?'

'No, I don't go in America, only sometimes in a long while. Mais je reste catholique. It's no good to change the religion.'

'On dit que Schmidt est catholique,' Fontan said.

'On dit, mais on ne sait jamais,' Madame Fontan said. 'I don't think Schmidt is catholique. There's not many catholique in America.'

'We are catholique,' I said.

'Sure, but you live in France,' Madame Fontan said. 'Je ne crois pas que Schmidt est catholique. Did he ever live in France?'

'Les Polacks sont catholiques,' Fontan said.

'That's true,' Madame Fontan said. 'They go to church, then they fight with knives all the way home and kill each other all day Sunday. But they're not real catholiques. They're Polack catholiques.'

'All catholiques are the same,' Fontan said. 'One catholique is like another.'

'I don't believe Schmidt is catholique,' Madame Fontan said. 'That's awfully funny if he's catholique. Moi, je ne crois pas.'

'Il est catholique,' I said.

'Schmidt is catholique,' Madame Fontan mused. 'I wouldn't have believed it. My God, il est catholique.'

'Marie va chercher de la bière,' Fontan said. 'Monsieur a soif – moi aussi.'

'Yes, all right,' Madame Fontan said from the next room. She went downstairs and we heard the stairs creaking. André sat reading in the corner. Fontan and I sat at the table, and he poured the beer from the last bottle into our two glasses, leaving a little in the bottom.

'C'est un bon pays pour la chasse,' Fontan said. 'J'aime beaucoup shooter les canards.'

'Mais il y a très bonne chasse aussi en France,' I said.

'C'est vrai,' Fontan said. 'Nous avons beaucoup de gibier là-bas.'

Madame Fontan came up the stairs with the beer bottles in her hands. 'Il est catholique,' she said. 'My God, Schmidt est catholique.'

'You think he'll be the President?' Fontan asked.

'No,' I said.

The next afternoon I drove out to Fontan's through the shade of the town, then along the dusty road, turning up the side road and leaving the car beside the fence. It was another hot day. Madame Fontan came to the back door. She looked like Mrs Santa Claus, clean and rosy-faced and white-haired and waddling when she walked.

'My God, hello,' she said. 'It's hot, my God.' She went back into the house to get some beer. I sat on the back porch and looked through the screen and the leaves of the tree at the heat and, away off, the mountains. There were furrowed brown mountains, and above them three peaks and a glacier with snow that you could see through the trees. The snow looked very white and pure and unreal. Madame Fontan came out and put down the bottles on the table.

'What do you see out there?'

'The snow.'

'C'est jolie, la neige.'

'Have a glass, too.'

'All right.'

She sat down on a chair beside me. 'Schmidt,' she said. 'If he's the President, you think we get the wine and beer all right?'

'Sure,' I said. 'Trust Schmidt.'

'Already we paid seven hundred fifty-five dollars in fines when they arrested Fontan. Twice the police arrested us and once the governments. All the money we made all the time Fontan worked in the mines and I did washing. We paid it all. They put Fontan in jail. Il n'a jamais fait de mal à personne.'

'He's a good man,' I said. 'It's a crime.'

'We don't charge too much money. The wine one dollar a litre. The beer ten cents a bottle. We never sell the beer before it's good. Lots of places they sell the beer right away when they make it, and then it gives everybody a headache. What's the matter with that? They put Fontan in jail and they take seven hundred fifty-five dollars.'

'It's wicked,' I said. 'Where is Fontan?'

'He stays with the wine. He has to watch it now to catch it just right,' she smiled. She did not think about the money any more. 'Vous savez, il est crazy pour le vin. Last night he brought a little bit home with him, what you drank, and a little bit of the new. The last new. It ain't ready yet, but he drank a little bit, and this morning he put a little bit in his coffee. Dans son café, vous savez? Il est crazy pour le vin! Il est comme ça. Son pays est comme ça. Where I live in the north they don't drink any wine. Everybody drinks beer. By where we lived there was a big brewery right near us. When I was a little girl I didn't like the smell of the hops in the carts. Nor in the fields. Je n'aime pas les houblons. No, my God, not a bit. The man that owns the brewery said to me and my sister to go to the brewery and drink the beer, and then we'd like the hops. That's true. Then we liked them all right. He had them give us the beer. We liked them all right then. But Fontan, il est crazy pour le vin. One time he killed a jack-rabbit and he wanted me to cook it with a sauce with wine, make a black sauce with wine and butter and mushrooms and onion and everything it it, for the jack. My God, I make the sauce all right, and he eat it all and said, "La sauce est meilleure que le jack." Dans son pays c'est comme ça. Il y a beaucoup de gibier et de vin. Moi, j'aime les pommes de terre, le saucisson, et la bière. C'est bon, la bière. C'est très bon pour la santé.'

'It's good,' I said. 'It and wine too.'

'You're like Fontan. But there was a thing here that I never saw. I don't think you've ever seen it either. There were Americans came here and they put whisky in the beer.'

'No,' I said.

'Oui. My God, yes, that's true. Et aussi une femme qui a vomis sur la table!'

'Comment?'

'C'est vrai. Elle a vomis sur la table. Et après elle a vomis dans ses shoes. And afterward they come back and say they want to come again and have another party the next Saturday, and I say no, my God, no! When they came I locked the door.'

'They're bad when they're drunk.'

'In the winter-time when the boys go to the dance they come in the cars and wait outside and say to Fontan, "Hey, Sam, sell us a bottle wine," or they buy the beer, and then they take the moonshine out of their pockets in a bottle and pour it in the beer and drink it. My God, that's the first time

I ever saw that in my life. They put whisky in the beer. My God, I don't understand *that*!'

'They want to get sick, so they'll know they're drunk.'

'One time a fellow comes here came to me and said he wanted me to cook them a big supper and they drink one two bottles of wine, and their girls come too, and then they go to the dance. All right, I said. So I made a big supper, and when they come already they drank a lot. Then they put whisky in the wine. My God, yes. I said to Fontan, "On va être malade!" "Oui," il dit. Then these girls were sick, nice girls, too, all-right girls. They were sick right at the table. Fontan tried to take them by the arm and show them where they could be sick all right in the cabinet, but the fellows said no, they were all right right there at the table.'

Fontan had come in. 'When they come again I locked the door. "No," I said. "Not for hundred fifty dollars." My God, no.'

'There is a word for such people when they do like that, in French,' Fontan said. He stood looking very old and tired from the heat.

'What?'

'Cochon,' he said delicately, hesitating to use such a strong word. 'They were like the cochon. C'est un mot très fort,' he apologized, 'mais vomir sur la table –' he shook his head sadly.

'Cochons,' I said. 'That's what they are – cochons. Salauds.'

The grossness of the words was distasteful to Fontan. He was glad to speak of something else.

'Il y a des gens très gentils, très sensibles, qui viennent aussi,' he said. 'There are officers from the fort. Very nice men. Good fellas. Everybody that was ever in France they want to come and drink wine. They like wine all right.'

'There was one man,' Madame Fontan said, 'and his wife never lets him get out. So he tells her he's tired, and goes to bed, and when she goes to the show he comes straight down here, sometimes in his pyjamas with just a coat over them. "Maria, some beer," he says, "for God's sake." He sits in his pyjamas and drinks the beer, and then he goes up to the fort and gets back in bed before his wife comes home from the show.'

'C'est un original,' Fontan said, 'mais vraiment gentil. He's a nice fella.'

'My God, yes, nice fella all right,' Madame Fontan said. 'He's always in bed when his wife gets back from the show.'

'I have to go away tomorrow,' I said. 'To the Crow Reservation. We go there for the opening of the prairie-chicken season.'

'Yes? You come back here before you go away. You come back here all right?'

'Absolutely.'

'Then the wine will be done,' Fontan said. 'We'll drink a bottle together.'

'Three bottles,' Madame Fontan said.

'I'll be back,' I said.

'We count on you,' Fontan said.

'Good night,' I said.

We got in early in the afternoon from the shooting-trip. We had been up that morning since five o'clock. The day before we had had good shooting, but that morning we had not seen a prairie-chicken. Riding in the open car, we were very hot and we stopped to eat our lunch out of the sun, under a tree beside the road. The sun was high and the patch of shade was very small. We ate sandwiches and crackers with sandwich filling on them, and were thirsty and tired, and glad when we finally were out and on the main road back to town. We came up behind a prairie-dog town and stopped the car to shoot at the prairie-dogs with the pistol. We shot two, but then stopped because the bullets that missed glanced off the rocks and the dirt, and sung off across the fields, and beyond the fields there were some trees along a watercourse, with a house, and we did not want to get in trouble from stray bullets going toward the house. So we drove on, and finally were on the road coming downhill toward the outlying houses of the town. Across the plain we could see the mountains. They were blue that day, and the snow on the high mountains shone like glass. The summer was ending, but the new snow had not yet come to stay on the high mountains; there was only the old sun-melted snow and the ice, and from a long way away it shone very brightly.

We wanted something cool and some shade. We were sun-burned and our lips blistered from the sun and alkali dust. We turned up the side road to Fontan's, stopped the car outside the house, and went in. It was cool inside the dining-room. Madame Fontan was alone.

'Only two bottles beer,' she said. 'It's all gone. The new is no good yet.'

I gave her some birds. 'That's good,' she said. 'All right. Thanks. That's good.' She went out to put the birds away where it was cooler. When we finished the beer I stood up. 'We have to go,' I said.

'You come back tonight all right? Fontan he's going to have the wine.'

'We'll come back before we go away.'

'You go away?'

'Yes. We have to leave in the morning.'

'That's too bad you go away. You come tonight. Fontan will have the wine. We'll make a fête before you go.'

'We'll come before we go.'

But that afternoon there were telegrams to send, the car to be gone over – a tyre had been cut by a stone and needed vulcanizing – and, without the car, I walked into the town, doing things that had to be done before we could go. When it was supper-time I was too tired to go out. We did not want a foreign language. All we wanted was to go early to bed.

As I lay in bed before I went to sleep, with all the things of summer piled around ready to be packed, the windows open and the air coming in cool from the mountains, I thought it was a shame not to have gone to Fontan's – but in a little while I was asleep. The next day we were busy all morning packing and ending the summer. We had lunch and were ready to start by two o'clock.

'We must go and say good-bye to the Fontans,' I said.

'Yes, we must.'

'I'm afraid they expected us last night.'

'I suppose we could have gone.'

'I wish we'd gone.'

We said good-bye to the man at the desk at the hotel, and to Larry and our other friends in the town, and then drove out to Fontan's. Both Monsieur and Madame were there. They were glad to see us. Fontan looked old and tired.

'We thought you would come last night,' Madame Fontan said. 'Fontan had three bottles of wine. When you did not come he drank it all up.'

'We can only stay a minute,' I said. 'We just came to say good-bye. We wanted to come last night. We intended to come, but we were too tired after the trip.'

'Go get some wine,' Fontan said.

'There is no wine. You drank it all up.'

Fontan looked very upset.

'I'll go get some,' he said. 'I'll just be gone a few minutes. I drank it up last night. We had it for you.'

'I knew you were tired. "My God," I said, "they're too tired all right to come",' Madame Fontan said. 'Go get some wine, Fontan.'

'I'll take you in the car,' I said.

'All right,' Fontan said. 'That way we'll go faster.'

We drove down the road in the motor car and turned up a side road about a mile away.

'You'll like that wine,' Fontan said. 'It's come out well. You can drink it for supper tonight.'

We stopped in front of a frame house. Fontan knocked on the door. There was no answer. We went around to the back. The back door was locked too. There were empty tin cans around the back door. We looked in the window. There was nobody inside. The kitchen was dirty and sloppy, but all the doors and windows were tight shut.

'That son of a bitch. Where is she gone out?' Fontan said. He was desperate.

'I know where I can get a key,' he said. 'You stay here.' I watched him go down to the next house down the road, knock on the door, talk to the woman who came out, and finally come back. He had a key. We tried it on the front door and the back, but it wouldn't work.

'That son of a bitch,' Fontan said. 'She's gone away somewhere.'

Looking through the window I could see where the wine was stored. Close to the window you could smell the inside of the house. It smelled sweet and sickish like an Indian house. Suddenly Fontan took a loose board and commenced digging at the earth beside the back door.

'I can get in,' he said. 'Son of a bitch, I can get in.'

There was a man in the back yard of the next house doing something to one of the front wheels of an old Ford.

'You better not,' I said. 'That man will see you. He's watching.'

Fontan straightened up. 'We'll try the key once more,' he said. We tried the key and it did not work. It turned half-way in either direction.

'We can't get in,' I said. 'We better go back.'

'I'll dig up the back,' Fontan offered.

'No, I wouldn't let you take the chance.'

'I'll do it.'

'No,' I said. 'That man would see. Then they would seize it.'

We went out to the car and drove back to Fontan's, stopping on the way to leave the key. Fontan did not say anything but swear in English. He was incoherent and crushed. We went in the house.

'That son of a bitch!' he said. 'We couldn't get the wine. My own wine that I made.'

All the happiness went from Madame Fontan's face. Fontan sat down in a corner with his head in his hands.

'We must go,' I said. 'It doesn't make any difference about the wine. You drink to us when we're gone.'

'Where did that crazy go?' Madame Fontan asked.

'I don't know,' Fontan said. 'I don't know where she go. Now you go away without any wine.'

'That's all right,' I said.

'That's no good,' Madame Fontan said. She shook her head.

'We have to go,' I said. 'Good-bye and good luck. Thank you for the fine times.'

Fontan shook his head. He was disgraced. Madame Fontan looked sad.

'Don't feel bad about the wine,' I said.

'He wanted you to drink his wine,' Madame Fontan said. 'You can come back next year?'

'No. Maybe the year after.'

'You see?' Fontan said to her.

'Good-bye,' I said. 'Don't think about the wine. Drink some for us when we're gone.' Fontan shook his head. He did not smile. He knew when he was ruined.

'That son of a bitch,' Fontan said to himself.

'Last night he had three bottles,' Madame Fontan said to comfort him. He shook his head.

'Good-bye,' he said.

Madame Fontan had tears in her eyes.

'Good-bye,' she said. She felt badly for Fontan.

'Good-bye,' we said, We all felt very badly. They stood in the doorway and we got in, and I started the motor. We waved. They stood together sadly on the porch. Fontan looked very old, and Madame Fontan looked sad. She waved to us and Fontan went in the house. We turned up the road.

'They felt so badly. Fontan felt terribly.'

'We ought to have gone last night.'

'Yes, we ought to have.'

We were through the town and out on the smooth road beyond, with the stubble of grain-fields on each side and the mountains off to the right. It looked like Spain, but it was Wyoming.

'I hope they have a lot of good luck.'

'They won't,' I said, 'and Schmidt won't be President either.'

The cement road stopped. The road was gravelled now and we left the plain and started up between two foothills; the road in a curve and commencing to climb. The soil of the hills was red, the sage grew in grey clumps, and as the road rose we could see across the hills and away across the plain of the valley to the mountains. They were farther now and they looked more like Spain than ever. The road curved and climbed again, and ahead there were some grouse dusting in the road. They flew as we came toward them, their wings beating fast, then sailing in long slants, and lit on the hillside below.

'They are so big and lovely. They're bigger than European partridges.'

'It's a fine country for la chasse, Fontan says.'

'And when the chasse is gone?'

'They'll be dead then.'

'The boy won't.'

'There's nothing to prove he won't,' I said.

'We ought to have gone last night.'

'Oh, yes,' I said. 'We ought to have gone.'

The Gambler, the Nun, and the Radio

They brought them in around midnight and then, all night long, everyone along the corridor heard the Russian.

'Where is he shot?' Mr Frazer asked the night nurse.

'In the thigh, I think.'

'What about the other one?'

'Oh, he's going to die, I'm afraid.'

'Where is he shot?'

'Twice in the abdomen. They only found one of the bullets.'

They were both beet workers, a Mexican and a Russian, and they were sitting drinking coffee in an all-night restaurant when someone came in the door and started shooting at the Mexican. The Russian crawled under a table and was hit, finally, by a stray shot fired at the Mexican as he lay on the floor with two bullets in his abdomen. That was what the paper said.

The Mexican told the police he had no idea who shot him. He believed it to be an accident.

'An accident that he fired eight shots at you and hit you twice, there?'

'Si, señor,' said the Mexican, who was named Cayetano Ruiz.

'An accident that he hit me at all, the cabron,' he said to the interpreter.

'What does he say?' asked the detective sergeant, looking across the bed at the interpreter.

'He says it was an accident.'

'Tell him to tell the truth, that he is going to die,' the detective said.

'Na,' said Cayetano. 'But tell him that I feel very sick and would prefer not to talk so much.'

'He says that he is telling the truth,' the interpreter said. Then, speaking confidently, to the detective, 'He don't know who shot him. They shot him in the back.'

'Yes,' said the detective. 'I understand that, but why did the bullets all go in the front?'

'Maybe he is spinning around,' said the interpreter.

'Listen,' said the detective, shaking his finger almost at Cayetano's nose, which projected, waxen yellow, from his dead-man's face in which his eyes were alive as a hawk's, 'I don't give a damn who shot you, but I've got to clear this thing up. Don't you want the man who shot you to be punished? Tell him that,' he said to the interpreter.

'He says to tell who shot you.'

'Mandarlo al carajo,' said Cayetano, who was very tired.

'He says he never saw the fellow at all,' the interpreter said. 'I tell you straight they shot him in the back.'

'Ask him who shot the Russian.'

'Poor Russian,' said Cayetano. 'He was on the floor with his head enveloped in his arms. He started to give cries when they shoot him and he is giving cries ever since. Poor Russian.'

'He says some fellow that he doesn't know. Maybe the same fellow that shot him.'

'Listen,' the detective said. 'This isn't Chicago. You're not a gangster. You don't have to act like a moving picture. It's all right to tell who shot you. Anybody would tell who shot them. That's all right to do. Suppose you don't tell who he is and he shoots somebody else. Suppose he shoots a woman or a child. You can't let him get away with that. You tell him,' he said to Mr Frazer. 'I don't trust that damn interpreter.'

'I am very reliable,' the interpreter said. Cayetano looked at Mr Frazer.

'Listen, amigo,' said Mr Frazer. 'The policeman says that we are not in Chicago but in Hailey, Montana. You are not a bandit and this has nothing to do with the cinema.'

'I believe him,' said Cayetano softly. 'Ya lo creo.'

'One can, with honour, denounce one's assailant. Everyone does it here, he says. He says what happens if after shooting you, this man shoots a woman or a child?'

'I am not married,' Cayetano said.

'He says any woman, any child.'

'The man is not crazy,' Cayetano said.

'He says you should denounce him,' Mr Frazer finished.

'Thank you,' Cayetano said. 'You are of the great translators. I speak English, but badly. I understand it all right. How did you break your leg?'

'A fall off a horse.'

'What bad luck. I am very sorry. Does it hurt much?'

'Not now. At first, yes.'

'Listen, amigo,' Cayetano began, 'I am very weak. You will pardon me. Also I have much pain; enough pain. It is very possible that I die. Please get this policeman out of here because I am very tired.' He made as though to roll to one side; then held himself still.

'I told him everything exactly as you said and he said to tell you, truly, that he doesn't know who shot him and that he is very weak and wishes you would question him later on,' Mr Frazer said.

'He'll probably be dead later on.'

'That's quite possible.'

'That's why I want to question him now.'

'Somebody shot him in the back, I tell you,' the interpreter said.

'Oh, for Chrisake,' the detective sergeant said, and put his note-book in his pocket.

Outside in the corridor the detective sergeant stood with the interpreter beside Mr Frazer's wheeled chair.

'I suppose you think somebody shot him in the back too?'

'Yes,' Frazer said. 'Somebody shot him in the back. What's it to you?'

'Don't get sore,' the sergeant said. 'I wish I could talk spick.'

'Why don't you learn?'

'You don't have to get sore. I don't get any fun out of asking that spick question. If I could talk spick it would be different.'

'You don't need to talk Spanish,' the interpreter said. 'I'm a very reliable interpreter.'

'Oh, for Chrisake,' the sergeant said. 'Well, so long. I'll come up and see you.'

'Thanks. I'm always in.'

'I guess you are all right. That was bad luck all right. Plenty bad luck.'

'It's coming along good now since he spliced the bone.'

'Yes, but it's a long time. A long, long time.'

'Don't let anybody shoot you in the back.'

'That's right,' he said. 'That's right. Well, I'm glad you're not sore.'

'So long,' said Mr Frazer.

Mr Frazer did not see Cayetano again for a long time, but each morning Sister Cecilia brought news of him. He was so uncomplaining she said and he was very bad now. He had peritonitis and they thought he could not live. Poor Cayetano, she said. He had such beautiful hands and such a fine face and he never complains. The odour, now, was really terrific. He would point to his nose with one finger and smile and shake his head, she said. He felt badly about the odour. It embarrassed him, Sister Cecilia said. Oh, he was such a fine patient. He always smiled. He wouldn't go to confession to Father but he promised to say his prayers, and not a Mexican had been to see him since he had been brought in. The Russian was going out at the end of the week. I could never feel anything about the Russian, Sister Cecilia said. Poor fellow, he suffered too. It was a greased bullet and dirty and the wound infected, but he made so much noise and then I always like the bad ones. That Cayetano, he's a bad one. Oh, he must really be a bad one, a thoroughly bad one, he's so fine and delicately made and he's never done any work with the hands. He's not a beet worker. I know he's not a beet worker. His hands are smooth and not a callous on them. I know he's a bad one of some sort. I'm going down and pray for him now. Poor Cayetano, he's having a dreadful time, and he doesn't make a sound. What did they have to shoot him·for? Oh, that poor Cayetano! I'm going right down and pray for him.

She went right down and prayed for him.

*

In that hospital a radio did not work very well until it was dusk. They said it was because there was so much ore in the ground or something about the mountains, but anyway it did not work well at all until it began to get dark outside; but all night it worked beautifully and when one station stopped you could go farther west and pick up another. The last one that you could get was Seattle, Washington, and due to the difference in time, when they signed off at four o'clock in the morning it was five o'clock in the morning in the hospital; and at six o'clock you could get the morning revellers in Minneapolis. That was on account of the difference in time, too, and Mr Frazer used to like to think of the morning revellers arriving at the studio and picture how they would look getting off a street car before daylight in the morning carrying their instruments. Maybe that was wrong and they kept their instruments at the place they revelled, but he always pictured them with their instruments. He had never been in Minneapolis and believed he probably would never go there, but he knew what it looked like that early in the morning.

Out of the window of the hospital you could see a field with tumbleweed coming out of the snow, and a bare clay butte. One morning the doctor wanted to show Mr Frazer two pheasants that were out there in the snow, and pulling the bed toward the window, the reading light fell off the iron bedstead and hit Mr Frazer on the head. This does not sound as funny now but it was very funny then. Everyone was looking out the window, and the doctor, who was a most excellent doctor, was pointing at the pheasants and pulling the bed toward the window, and then, just as in a comic section, Mr Frazer was knocked out by the leaded base of the lamp hitting the top of his head. It seemed the antithesis of healing or whatever people were in the hospital for, and everyone thought it was very funny, as a joke on Mr Frazer and on the doctor. Everything is much simpler in hospital, including the jokes.

From the other window, if the bed was turned, you could see the town, with a little smoke above it, and the Dawson mountains looking like real mountains with the winter snow on them. Those were the two views since the wheeled chair had proved to be premature. It is really best to be in bed if you are in hospital; since two views, with time to observe them, from a room the temperature of which you control, are much better than any number of views seen for a few minutes from hot, empty rooms that are waiting for someone else, or just abandoned, which you are wheeled in and out of. If you stay long enough in a room the view, whatever it is, acquires a great value and becomes very important and you would not change it, not even by a different angle. Just as, with the radio, there are certain things that you become fond of, and you welcome them and resent the new things. The best tunes they had that winter were 'Sing Something Simple', 'Singsong Girl' and 'Little White Lies'. No other tunes were as satisfactory, Mr Frazer felt. 'Betty Co-ed' was a good tune too, but the parody of the words which came unavoidably into Mr Frazer's mind grew so steadily and increasingly obscene that, there being no one to appreciate it, he finally abandoned it and let the song go back to football.

About nine o'clock in the morning they would start using the X-ray machine, and then the radio, which, by then was only getting Hailey, became useless. Many people in Hailey who owned radios protested about the hospital's X-ray machine which ruined their morning reception, but there was never any action taken, although many felt it was a shame the hospital could not use their machine at a time when people were not using their radios.

About the time when it became necessary to turn off the radio Sister Cecilia came in.

'How's Cayetano, Sister Cecilia?' Mr Frazer asked.

'Oh, he's very bad.'

'Is he out of his head?'

'No, but I'm afraid he's going to die.'

'How are you?'

'I'm very worried about him, and do you know that absolutely no one has come to see him? He could die just like a dog for all those Mexicans care. They're really dreadful.'

'Do you want to come up and hear the game this afternoon?'

'Oh, no,' she said. 'I'd be too excited. I'll be in the chapel praying.'

'We ought to be able to hear it pretty well,' Mr Frazer said. 'They're playing out on the coast and the difference in time will bring it late enough so we can get it all right.'

'Oh, no. I couldn't do it. The world series nearly finished me. When the Athletics were at bat I was praying right out loud: "Oh, Lord, direct their batting eyes! Oh, Lord, may he hit one! Oh, Lord, may he hit safely!" Then when they filled the bases in the third game, you remember, it was too much for me. "Oh, Lord, may he hit it out of the lot! Oh, Lord, may he drive it clean over the fence!" Then you know when the Cardinals would come to bat it was simply dreadful. "Oh, Lord, may they not see it! Oh, Lord, don't let them even catch a glimpse of it. Oh, Lord, may they fan!" And this game is even worse. It's Notre Dame. Our Lady. No, I'll be in the chapel. For Our Lady. They're playing for Our Lady. I wish you'd write something sometime for Our Lady. You could do it. You know you could do it, Mr Frazer.'

'I don't know anything about here that I could write. It's mostly been written already,' Mr Frazer said. 'You wouldn't like the way I write. She wouldn't care for it either.'

'You'll write about her sometimes,' Sister said. 'I know you will. You must write about Our Lady.'

'You'd better come up and hear the game.'

'It would be too much for me. No, I'll be in the chapel doing what I can.'

That afternoon they had been playing about five minutes when a probationer came into the room and said, 'Sister Cecilia wants to know how the game is going?'

'Tell her they have a touchdown already.'

In a little while the probationer came into the room again.

'Tell her they're playing them off their feet,' Mr Frazer said.

A little later he rang the bell for the nurse who was on floor duty. 'Would you mind going down to the chapel or sending word to Sister Cecilia that Notre Dame has them fourteen to nothing at the end of the first quarter and that it's all right. She can stop praying.'

In a few minutes Sister Cecilia came into the room. She was very excited. 'What does fourteen to nothing mean? I don't know anything about this game. That's a nice safe lead in baseball. But I don't know anything about football. It may not mean a thing. I'm going right back down to the chapel and pray until it's finished.'

'They have them beaten,' Frazer said. 'I promise you. Stay and listen with me.'

'No. No. No. No. No. No. No,' she said. 'I'm going right down to the chapel to pray.'

Mr Frazer sent down word whenever Notre Dame scored, and finally, when it had been dark a long time, the final result.

'How's Sister Cecilia?'

'They're all at chapel,' she said.

The next morning Sister Cecilia came in. She was very pleased and confident.

'I knew they couldn't beat Our Lady,' she said. 'They couldn't. Cayetano's better too. He's much better. He's going to have visitors. He can't see them yet, but they are going to come and that will make him feel better and know he's not forgotten by his own people. I went down and saw that O'Brien boy at Police Headquarters and told him that he's got to send some Mexicans up to see poor Cayetano. He's going to send some this afternoon. Then that poor man will feel better. It's wicked the way no one has come to see him.'

That afternoon about five o'clock three Mexicans came into the room.

'Can one?' asked the biggest one, who had very thick lips and was quite fat.

'Why not?' Mr Frazer answered. 'Sit down, gentlemen. Will you take something?'

'Many thanks,' said the big one.

'Thanks,' said the darkest and smallest one.

'Thanks, no,' said the thin one. 'It mounts to my head.' He tapped his head.

The nurse brought some glasses. 'Please give them the bottle,' Frazer said. 'It is from Red Lodge,' he explained.

'That of Red Lodge is the best,' said the big one. 'Much better than that of Big Timber.'

'Clearly,' said the smallest one, 'and costs more too.'

'In Red Lodge it is of all prices,' said the big one.

'How many tubes has the radio?' asked the one who did not drink.

'Seven.'

'Very beautiful,' he said. 'What does it cost?'

'I don't know,' Mr Frazer said. 'It is rented.'

'You gentlemen are friends of Cayetano?'

'No,' said the big one. 'We are friends of he who wounded him.'

'We were sent here by the police,' the smallest one said.

'We have a little place,' the big one said. 'He and I,' indicating the one who did not drink. 'He has a little place too,' indicating the small, dark one. 'The police tell us we have to come – so we came.'

'I am very happy you have come.'

'Equally,' said the big one.

'Will you have another little cup?'

'Why not?' said the big one.

'With your permission,' said the smallest one.

'Not me,' said the thin one. 'It mounts to my head.'

'It is very good,' said the smallest one.

'Why not try some?' Mr Frazer asked the thin one. 'Let a little mount to your head.'

'Afterwards comes the headache,' said the thin one.

'Could you not send friends of Cayetano to see him?' Frazer asked.

'He has no friends.'

'Every man has friends.'

'This one, no.'

'What does he do?'

'He is a card-player.'

'Is he good?'

'I believe it.'

'From me,' said the smallest one, 'he won one hundred and

eighty dollars. Now there is no longer one hundred and eighty dollars in the world.'

'From me,' said the thin one, 'he won two hundred and eleven dollars. Fix yourself on that figure.'

'I never played with him,' said the fat one.

'He must be very rich,' Mr Frazer suggested.

'He is poorer than we,' said the little Mexican. 'He has no more than the shirt on his back.'

'And that shirt is of little value now,' Mr Frazer said. 'Perforated as it is.'

'Clearly.'

'The one who wounded him was a card-player?'

'No, a beet worker. He has had to leave town.'

'Fix yourself on this,' said the smallest one. 'He was the best guitar player ever in this town. The finest.'

'What a shame.'

'I believe it,' said the biggest one. 'How he could touch the guitar.'

'There are no good guitar players left?'

'Not the shadow of a guitar player.'

'There is an accordion player who is worth something,' the thin man said.

'There are a few who touch various instruments,' the big one said. 'You like music?'

'How would I not?'

'We will come one night with music? You think the sister would allow it? She seems very amiable.'

'I am sure she would permit it when Cayetano is able to hear it.'

'Is she a little crazy?' asked the thin one.

'Who?'

'That sister.'

'No,' Mr Frazer said. 'She is a fine woman of great intelligence and sympathy.'

'I distrust all priests, monks and sisters,' said the thin one.

'He had bad experiences when a boy,' the smallest one said.

'I was an acolyte,' the thin one said proudly. 'Now I believe in nothing. Neither do I go to mass.'

'Why? Does it mount to your head?'

'No,' said the thin one. 'It is alcohol that mounts to my head. Religion is the opium of the poor.'

'I thought marijuana was the opium of the poor,' Frazer said.

'Did you ever smoke opium?' the big one asked.

'No.'

'Nor I,' he said. 'It seems it is very bad. One commences and cannot stop. It is a vice.'

'Like religion,' said the thin one.

'This one,' said the smallest Mexican, 'is very strong against religion.'

'It is necessary to be very strong against something,' Mr Frazer said politely.

'I respect those who have faith even though they are ignorant,' the thin one said.

'Good,' said Mr Frazer.

'What can we bring you?' asked the big Mexican. 'Do you lack for anything?'

'I would be glad to buy some beer if there is good beer.'

'We will bring beer.'

'Another copita before you go?'

'It is very good.'

'We are robbing you.'

'I can't take it. It goes to my head. Then I have a bad headache and sick at the stomach.'

'Good-bye, gentlemen.'

'Good-bye and thanks.'

They went out and there was supper and then the radio, turned to be as quiet as possible and still be heard, and the stations finally signing off in this order: Denver, Salt Lake City, Los Angeles and Seattle. Mr Frazer received no picture of Denver from the radio. He could see Denver from the *Denver Post*, and correct the picture from the *Rocky Mountain News*. Nor did he ever have any feel of Salt Lake City or Los Angeles from what he heard from those places. All he felt about Salt Lake City was that it was clean, but dull, and there were too many ballrooms mentioned in too many big hotels for him to see Los Angeles. He could not feel it for the ball-rooms. But Seattle he came to know very well, the taxicab company with the big white cabs (each cab equipped with radio itself) he rode in every night out to the roadhouse on the Canadian side where he followed the course of parties by the musical selections they phoned for. He lived in Seattle from two o'clock on, each night, hearing the pieces that all the different people asked for, and it was as real as Minneapolis, where the revellers left their beds each morning to make the trip down to the studio. Mr Frazer grew very fond of Seattle, Washington.

The Mexicans came and brought beer but it was not good beer. Mr Frazer saw them but he did not feel like talking and when they went he knew they would not come again. His nerves had become tricky and he disliked seeing people while he was in this condition. His nerves went bad at the end of five weeks, and while he was pleased they lasted that long yet he resented being forced to make the same experiment when he already knew the answer. Mr Frazer had been through this all before. The only thing which was new to him was the radio. He played it all night long, turned so low he could barely hear it, and he was learning to listen to it without thinking.

Sister Cecilia came into the room about ten o'clock in the morning on that day and brought the mail. She was very handsome, and Mr Frazer liked to see her and to hear her talk, but the mail, supposedly coming from a different world, was important. However, there was nothing in the mail of any interest.

'You look *so* much better,' she said. 'You'll be leaving us soon.'

'Yes,' Mr Frazer said. 'You look very happy this morning.'

'Oh, I am. This morning I feel as though I might be a saint.'

Mr Frazer was a little taken aback at this.

'Yes,' Sister Cecilia went on. 'That's what I want to be. A saint. Ever since I was a little girl I've wanted to be a saint. When I was a girl I thought if I renounced the world and went into the convent I would be a saint. That was what I wanted to be and that was what I thought I had to do to be one. I expected I would be a saint. I was absolutely sure I would be one. For just a moment I thought I was one. I was so happy and it seemed so simple and easy. When I awoke in the morning I expected I would be a saint, but I wasn't. I've never become one. I want so to be one. All I want is to be a saint. That is all I've ever wanted. And this morning I feel as though I might be one. Oh, I hope I will get to be one.'

'You'll be one. Everybody gets what they want. That's what they always tell me.'

'I don't know now. When I was a girl it seemed so simple. I knew I would be a saint. Only I believed it took time when I found it did not happen suddenly. Now it seems almost impossible.'

'I'd say you had a good chance.'

'Do you really think so? No, I don't want just to be encouraged. Don't just encourage me. I want to be a saint. I want to be a saint.'

'Of course you'll be a saint,' Mr Frazer said.

'No, probably I won't be. But, oh, if I could only be a saint! I'd be perfectly happy.'

'You're three to one to be a saint.'

'No, don't encourage me. But, oh, if I could only be a saint! If I could only be a saint!'

'How's your friend Cayetano?'

'He's going to get well, but he's paralysed. One of the bullets hit the big nerve that goes down through his thigh and that leg is paralysed. They only found it out when he got well enough so that he could move.'

'Maybe the nerve will regenerate.'

'I'm praying that it will,' Sister Cecilia said. 'You ought to see him.'

'I don't feel like seeing anybody.'

'You know you'd like to see him. They could wheel him in here.'

'All right.'

They wheeled him in, thin, his skin transparent, his hair

black and needing to be cut, his eyes very laughing, his teeth bad when he smiled.

'Hola, amigo! Que tal?'

'As you see,' said Mr Frazer. 'And thou?'

'Alive and with the leg paralysed.'

'Bad,' Mr Frazer said. 'But the nerve can regenerate and be as good as new.'

'So they tell me.'

'What about the pain?'

'Not now. For a while I was crazy with it in the belly. I thought the pain alone would kill me.'

Sister Cecilia was observing them happily.

'She tells me you never made a sound,' Mr Frazer said.

'So many people in the ward,' the Mexican said deprecatingly. 'What class of pain do you have?'

'Big enough. Clearly not as bad as yours. When the nurse goes out I cry an hour, two hours. It rests me. My nerves are bad now.'

'You have the radio. If I had a private room and a radio I would be crying and yelling all night long.'

'I doubt it.'

'Hombre, si. It's very healthy. But you cannot do it with so many people.'

'At least,' Mr Frazer said, 'the hands are still good. They tell me you make your living with the hands.'

'And the head,' he said, tapping his forehead. 'But the head isn't worth as much.'

'Three of your countrymen were here.'

'Sent by the police to see me.'

'They brought some beer.'

'It probably was bad.'

'It was bad.'

'Tonight, sent by the police, they come to serenade me.' He laughed, then tapped his stomach. 'I cannot laugh yet. As musicians they are fatal.'

'And the one who shot you?'

'Another fool. I won thirty-eight dollars from him at cards. That is not to kill about.'

'The three told me you win much money.'

'And am poorer than the birds.'

'How?'

'I am a poor idealist. I am the victim of illusions.' He laughed, then grinned and tapped his stomach. 'I am a professional gambler but I like to gamble. To really gamble. Little gambling is all crooked. For real gambling you need luck. I have no luck.'

'Never?'

'Never. I am completely without luck. Look, this cabron who shoots me just now. Can he shoot? No. The first shot he fires into nothing. The second is intercepted by a poor Russian. That would seem to be luck. What happens? He shoots me twice in the belly. He is a lucky man. I have no luck. He could not hit a horse if he were holding the stirrup. All luck.'

'I thought he shot you first and the Russian after.'

'No, the Russian first, me after. The paper was mistaken.'

'Why didn't you shoot him?'

'I never carry a gun. With my luck, if I carried a gun I would be hanged ten times a year. I am a cheap card player, only that.' He stopped, then continued. 'When I make a sum of money I gamble and when I gamble I lose. I have passed at dice for three thousand dollars and crapped out for the six. With good dice. More than once.'

'Why continue?'

'If I live long enough the luck will change. I have bad luck now for fifteen years. If I ever get any good luck I will be rich.' He grinned. 'I am a good gambler, really I would enjoy being rich.'

'Do you have bad luck with all games?'

'With everything and with women.' He smiled again, showing his bad teeth.

'Truly?'

'Truly.'

'And what is there to do?'

'Continue, slowly, and wait for luck to change.'

'But with women?'

'No gambler has luck with women. He is too concentrated. He works nights. When he should be with the woman. No man who works nights can hold a woman if the woman is worth anything.'

'You are a philosopher.'

'No, hombre. A gambler of the small towns. One small town, then another, another, then a big town, then start over again.'

'Then shot in the belly.'

'The first time,' he said. 'That has only happened once.'

'I tire you talking?' Mr Frazer suggested.

'No,' he said. 'I must tire you.'

'And the leg?'

'I have no great use for the leg. I am all right with the leg or not. I will be able to circulate.'

'I wish you luck, truly, and with all my heart,' Mr Frazer said.

'Equally,' he said. 'And that the pain stops.'

'It will not last, certainly. It is passing. It is of no importance.'

'That it passes quickly.'

'Equally.'

That night the Mexicans played the accordion and other instruments in the ward and it was cheerful and the noise of the inhalations and exhalations of the accordion, and of the bells, the traps and the drum came down the corridor. In that ward there was a rodeo rider who had come out of the chutes on Midnight on a hot dusty afternoon with the big crowd watching, and now, with a broken back, was going to learn to work in leather and to cane chairs when he got well enough to leave the hospital. There was a carpenter who had fallen with a scaffolding and broken both ankles and both wrists. He had lit like a cat but without a cat's resiliency. They could fix him up so that he could work again but it would take a long time. There was a boy from a farm, about sixteen years old, with a broken leg that had been badly set and was to be rebroken. There was Cayetano Ruiz, a small-town gambler with a paralysed leg. Down the corridor Mr Frazer could hear them all laughing and merry with the music made by the Mexicans who had been sent by the police. The Mexicans were having a good time. They came in, very excited, to see Mr Frazer and wanted to know if there was anything he wanted them to play, and they came twice more to play at night of their own accord.

The last time they played Mr Frazer lay in his room with the door open and listened to the noisy, bad music and could not keep from thinking. When they wanted to know what he wished played, he asked for the 'Cucaracha', which has the sinister lightness and deftness of so many of the tunes men have gone to die to. They played noisily and with emotion. The tune was better than most of such tunes, to Mr Frazer's mind, but the effect was all the same.

In spite of this introduction of emotion, Mr Frazer went on thinking. Usually he avoided thinking all he could, except when he was writing, but now he was thinking about those who were playing and what the little one had said.

Religion is the opium of the people. He believed that, that dyspeptic little joint-keeper. Yes, and music is the opium of the people. Old mount-to-the-head hadn't thought of that. And now economics is the opium of the people; along with patriotism the opium of the people in Italy and Germany. What about sexual intercourse, was that an opium of the people? Of some of the people. Of some of the best of the people. But drink was a sovereign opium of the people, oh, an excellent opium. Although some prefer the radio, another opium of the people, a cheap one he had just been using. Along with these went gambling, an opium of the people if there ever was one, one of the oldest. Ambition was another, an opium of the people, along with a belief in any new form of government. What you wanted was the minimum of government, always less government. Liberty, what we believed in, now the name of a MacFadden publication. We believed in that although they had not found a new name for it yet. But what was the real one? What was the real, the actual, opium of the people? He knew it very well. It was gone just a little way around the corner in that well-lighted part of his mind that was there after two or more drinks in the evening; that he knew was there (it was not really there of course). What was it? He knew very well. What was it? Of course; bread was the opium of the people. Would he remember that and would it make sense in the daylight? Bread is the opium of the people.

'Listen,' Mr Frazer said to the nurse when she came. 'Get that little thin Mexican in here, will you please?'

'How do you like it?' the Mexican said at the door.

'Very much.'

'It is a historic tune,' the Mexican said. 'It is the tune of the real revolution.'

'Listen,' said Mr Frazer. 'Why should the people be operated on without an anaesthetic?'

'I do not understand.'

'Why are not all the opiums of the people good? What do you want to do with the people?'

'They should be rescued from ignorance.'

'Don't talk nonsense. Education is an opium of the people. You ought to know that. You've had a little.'

'You do not believe in education?'

'No,' said Mr Frazer. 'In knowledge, yes.'

'I do not follow you.'

'Many times I do not follow myself with pleasure.'

'You want to hear the "Cucaracha" another time?' asked the Mexican worriedly.

'Yes,' said Mr Frazer. 'Play the "Cucaracha" another time. It's better than the radio.'

Revolution, Mr Frazer thought, is no opium. Revolution is a catharsis; an ecstasy which can only be prolonged by tyranny. The opiums are for before and for after. He was thinking well, a little too well.

They would go now in a little while, he thought, and they would take the 'Cucaracha' with them. Then he would have a little spot of the giant killer and play the radio, you could play the radio so that you could hardly hear it.

Fathers and Sons

There had been a sign to detour in the centre of the main street of this town, but cars had obviously gone through, so, believing it was some repair which had been completed, Nicholas Adams drove on through the town along the empty, brick-paved street, stopped by traffic lights that flashed on and off on this traffic-less Sunday, and would be gone next year when the payments on the system were not met; on under the heavy trees of the small town that are a part of your heart if it is your town and you have walked under them, but that are only too heavy, that shut out the sun and that dampen the houses for a stranger; out past the last house and on to the highway that rose and fell straight away ahead with banks of red dirt sliced cleanly away and the second-growth timber on both sides. It was not his country but it was the middle of fall and all of this country was good to drive through and to see. The cotton was picked and in the clearings there were patches of corn, some cut with streaks of red sorghum, and, driving easily, his son asleep on the seat by his side, the day's run made, knowing the town he would reach for the night, Nick noticed which cornfields had soy beans or peas in them, how the thickets and the cut-over land lay, where the cabins and houses were in relation to the fields and the thickets; hunting the country in his mind as he went by; sizing up each clearing as to feed and cover and figuring where you would find a covey and which way they would fly.

In shooting quail you must not get between them and their habitual cover, once the dogs have found them, or when they flush they will come pouring at you, some rising steep, some skimming by your ears, whirring into a size you have never seen them in the air as they pass, the only way being to turn and take them over your shoulder as they go, before they set their wings and angle down into the thicket. Hunting this country for quail as his father taught him, Nicholas Adams started thinking about his father. When he first thought about him it was always the eyes. The big frame, the quick movements, the wide shoulders, the hooked, hawk nose, the beard that covered the weak chin, you never thought about – it was always the eyes. They were protected in his head by the formation of the brows; set deep as though a special protection had been devised for some very valuable instrument. They saw much farther and much quicker than the human eye sees and they were the great gift his father had. His father saw as a big-horn ram or as an eagle sees, literally.

He would be standing with his father on one shore of the lake, his own eyes were very good then, and his father would say, 'They've run up the flag.' Nick would not see the flag at the flag pole. 'There,' his father would say, 'it's your sister Dorothy. She's got the flag up and she's walking out on to the dock.'

Nick would look across the lake and he could see the long wooded shore-line, the higher timber behind, the point that guarded the bay, the clear hills of the farm and the white of their cottage in the trees, but he could not see any flag pole, or any dock, only the white of the beach and the curve of the shore.

'Can you see the sheep on the hillside toward the point?'

'Yes.'

They were a whitish patch on the grey-green of the hill.

'I can count them,' his father said.

Like all men with a faculty that surpasses human requirements, his father was very nervous. Then, too, he was sentimental, and, like most sentimental people, he was both cruel and abused. Also, he had much bad luck, and it was not all of it his own. He had died in a trap that he had helped only a little to set, and they had all betrayed him in their various ways before he died. All sentimental people are betrayed so many times. Nick could not write about him yet, although he would, later, but the quail country made him remember him as he was when Nick was a boy and he was very grateful to him for two things: fishing and shooting. His father was as sound on those two things as he was unsound on sex, for instance, and Nick was glad that it had been that way; for someone has to give you your first gun or the opportunity to get it and use it, and you have to live where there is game or fish if you are to learn about them, and now, at thirty-eight, he loved to fish and to shoot exactly as much as when he first had gone with his father. It was a passion that had never slackened and he was very grateful to his father for bringing him to know it.

While for the other, that his father was not sound about, all the equipment you will ever have is provided and each man learns all there is for him to know about it without advice: and it makes no difference where you live. He remembered very clearly the only two pieces of information his father had given him about that. Once when they were out shooting together Nick shot a red squirrel out of a hemlock tree. The squirrel fell, wounded, and when Nick picked him up bit the boy clean through the ball of the thumb.

'The dirty little bugger,' Nick said and smacked the squirrel's head against the tree. 'Look how he bit me.'

His father looked and said, 'Suck it out clean and put some iodine on when you get home.'

'The little bugger,' Nick said.

'Do you know what a bugger is?' his father asked him.

'We call anything a bugger,' Nick said.

'A bugger is a man who has intercourse with animals.'

'Why?' Nick said.

'I don't know,' his father said. 'But it is a heinous crime.'

Nick's imagination was both stirred and horrified by this and he thought of various animals but none seemed attractive or practical and that was the sum total of direct sexual knowledge bequeathed him by his father except on one other subject. One morning he read in the paper that Enrico Caruso had been arrested for mashing.

'What is mashing?'

'It is one of the most heinous crimes,' his father answered. Nick's imagination pictured the great tenor doing something strange, bizarre and heinous with a potato masher to a beautiful lady who looked like the pictures of Anna Held on the inside of cigar boxes. He resolved, with considerable horror, that when he was old enough he would try mashing at least once.

His father had summed up the whole matter by stating that masturbation produced blindness, insanity and death, while a man who went with prostitutes would contract hideous venereal diseases and that the thing to do was to keep your hands off of people. On the other hand his father had the finest pair of eyes he had ever seen and Nick had loved him very much and for a long time. Now, knowing how it had all been, even remembering the earliest times before things had gone badly was not good remembering. If he wrote it he could get rid of it. He had gotten rid of many things by writing them. But it was still too early for that. There were still too many people. So he decided to think of something else. There was nothing to do about his father and he had thought it all through many times. The handsome job the undertaker had done on his father's face had not blurred in his mind and all the rest of it was quite clear, including the responsibilities. He had complimented the undertaker. The undertaker had been both proud and smugly pleased. But it was not the undertaker that had given him that last face. The undertaker had only made certain dashingly executed repairs of doubtful artistic merit. The face had been making itself and being made for a long time. It had modelled fast in the last three years. It was a good story but there were still too many people alive for him to write it.

Nick's own education in those earlier matters had been acquired in the hemlock woods behind the Indian camp. This was reached by a trail which ran from the cottage through the woods to the farm and then by a road which wound through the slashings to the camp. Now if he could feel all of that trail with bare feet. First there was the pine-needle loam through the hemlock woods behind the cottage where the fallen logs crumbled into wood dust and long splintered pieces of wood hung like javelins in the trees that had been struck by lightning. You crossed the creek on a log and if you stepped off there was the black muck of the swamp. You climbed a fence out of the woods and the trail was hard in the sun across the field with cropped grass and sheep sorrel and mullen growing and to the left the quaky bog of the creek bottom where the killdeer plover fed. The spring house was in that creek. Below the barn there was fresh warm manure and the other old manure was caked dry on top. Then there was another fence and the hard, hot trail from the barn to the house and the hot sandy road that ran down to the woods, crossing the creek, on a bridge this time, where the cat-tails grew that you soaked in kerosene to make jacklights with for spearing fish at night.

Then the main road went off to the left, skirting the woods and climbing the hill, while you went into the woods on the wide clay and shale road, cool under the trees, and broadened for them to skid out the hemlock bark the Indians cut. The hemlock bark was piled in long rows of stacks, roofed over with more bark, like houses, and the peeled logs lay huge and yellow where the trees had been felled. They left the logs in the woods to rot, they did not even clear away or burn the tops. It was only the bark they wanted for the tannery at Boyne City; hauling it across the lake on the ice in winter, and each year there was less forest and more open, hot, shadeless, weed-grown slashing.

But there was still much forest then, virgin forest where the trees grew high before there were any branches and you walked on the brown, clean, springy-needled ground with no undergrowth and it was cool on the hottest days and they three lay against the trunk of a hemlock wider than two beds are long, with the breeze high in the tops and the cool light that came in patches, and Billy said:

'You want Trudy again?'

'You want to?'

'Uh Huh.'

'Come on.'

'No, here.'

'But Billy –'

'I no mind Billy. He my brother.'

Then afterwards they sat, the three of them, listening for a black squirrel that was in the top branches where they could not see him. They were waiting for him to bark again because when he barked he would jerk his tail and Nick would shoot where he saw any movement. His father gave him only three cartridges a day to hunt with and he had a single-barrel twenty-gauge shotgun with a very long barrel.

'Son of a bitch never move,' Billy said.

'You shoot, Nickie. Scare him. We see him jump. Shoot him again,' Trudy said. It was a long speech for her.

'I've only got two shells,' Nick said.

'Son of a bitch,' said Billy.

They sat against the tree and were quiet. Nick was feeling hollow and happy.

'Eddie says he going to come some night to sleep in bed with your sister Dorothy.'

'What?'

'He said.'

Trudy nodded.

'That's all he want to do,' she said. Eddie was their older half-brother. He was seventeen.

'If Eddie Gilby ever comes at night and even speaks to Dorothy you know what I'd do to him? I'd kill him like this.' Nick cocked the gun and hardly taking aim pulled the trigger, blowing a hole as big as your hand in the head or belly of that half-breed bastard Eddie Gilby. 'Like that. I'd kill him like that.'

'He better not come then,' Trudy said. She put her hand in Nick's pocket.

'He'd better watch out plenty,' said Billy.

'He's a big bluff.' Trudy was exploring with her hand in Nick's pocket. 'But don't you kill him. You get plenty trouble.'

'I'd kill him like that,' Nick said. Eddie Gilby lay on the ground with all his chest shot away. Nick put his foot on him proudly.

'I'd scalp him,' he said happily.

'No,' said Trudy. 'That's dirty.'

'I'd scalp him and send it to his mother.'

'His mother dead,' Trudy said. 'Don't you kill him, Nickie. Don't you kill him for me.'

'After I scalped him I'd throw him to the dogs.'

Billy was very depressed. 'He better watch out,' he said gloomily.

'They'd tear him to pieces,' Nick said, pleased with the picture. Then, having scalped that half-breed renegade and standing, watching the dogs tear him, his face unchanging, he fell backward against the tree, held tight around the neck, Trudy holding him, choking him, and crying, 'No kill him! No kill him! No kill him! No. No. No. Nickie. Nickie. Nickie!'

'What's the matter with you?'

'No kill him.'

'I got to kill him.'

'He's just a big bluff.'

'All right,' Nickie said. 'I won't kill him unless he comes around the house. Let go of me.'

'That's good,' Trudy said. 'You want to do anything now? I feel good now.'

'If Billy goes away.' Nick had killed Eddie Gilby, then pardoned him his life, and he was a man now.

'You go, Billy. You hang around all the time. Go on.'

'Son a bitch,' Billy said. 'I get tired this. What we come? Hunt or what?'

'You can take the gun. There's one shell.'

'All right. I get a big black one all right.'

'I'll holler,' Nick said.

Then, later, it was a long time after and Billy was still away.

'You think we make a baby?' Trudy folded her brown legs together happily and rubbed against him. Something inside Nick had gone a long way away.

'I don't think so,' he said.

'Make plenty baby what the hell.'

They heard Billy shoot.

'I wonder if he got one.'

'Don't care,' said Trudy.

Billy came through the trees. He had the gun over his shoulder and he held a black squirrel by the front paws.

'Look,' he said, 'bigger than a cat. You all through?'

'Where'd you get him?'

'Over there. Saw him jump first.'

'Got to go home,' Nick said.

'No,' said Trudy.

'I got to get there for supper.'

'All right.'

'Want to hunt tomorrow?'

'All right.'

'You can have the squirrel.'

'All right.'

'Come out after supper?'

'No.'

'How you feel?'

'Good.'

'All right.'

'Give me kiss on the face,' said Trudy.

Now, as he rode along the highway in the car and it was getting dark, Nick was all through thinking about his father. The end of the day never made him think of him. The end of the day had always belonged to Nick alone and he never felt right unless he was alone at it. His father came back to him in the fall of the year, or in the early spring when there had been jacksnipe on the prairie, or when he saw shocks of corn, or when he saw a lake, or if he ever saw a horse and buggy, or when he saw, or heard, wild geese, or in a duck blind; remembering the time an eagle dropped through the whirling snow to strike a canvas-covered decoy, rising, his wings beating, the talons caught in the canvas. His father was with him, suddenly, in deserted orchards and in new-ploughed fields, in thickets, on small hills, or when going through dead grass, whenever splitting wood or hauling water, by grist mills, cider mills and dams and always with open fires. The towns he lived in were not towns his father knew. After he was fifteen he had shared nothing with him.

His father had frost in his beard in cold weather and in hot weather he sweated very much. He liked to work in the sun on the farm because he did not have to and he loved manual work, which Nick did not. Nick loved his father but hated the smell of him and once when he had to wear a suit of his father's underwear that had gotten too small for his father it made him feel sick and he took it off and put it under two stones in the creek and said that he had lost it. He had told his father how it was when his father had made him put it on but his father had said it was freshly washed. It had been, too. When Nick had asked him to smell of it his father sniffed at it indignantly and said that it was clean and fresh. When Nick came home from fishing without it and said he lost it he was whipped for lying.

Afterwards he had sat inside the woodshed with the door open, his shotgun loaded and cocked, looking across at his father sitting on the screen porch reading the paper, and thought, 'I can blow him to hell. I can kill him.' Finally he felt his anger go out of him and he felt a little sick about it being the gun that his father had given him. Then he had gone to the Indian camp, walking there in the dark, to get rid of the smell. There was only one person in his family that he liked the smell of; one sister. All the others he avoided all contact with. That sense blunted when he started to smoke. It was a good thing. It was good for a bird dog but it did not help a man.

'What was it like, Papa, when you were a little boy and used to hunt with the Indians?'

'I don't know,' Nick was startled. He had not even noticed the boy was awake. He looked at him sitting beside him on the seat. He had felt quite alone but this boy had been with him. He wondered for how long. 'We used to go all day to hunt black squirrels,' he said. 'My father only gave me three shells a day because he said that would teach me to hunt and it wasn't good for a boy to go banging around. I went with a boy named Billy Gilby and his sister Trudy. We used to go out nearly every day all one summer.'

'Those are funny names for Indians.'

'Yes, aren't they,' Nick said.

'But tell me what they were like.'

'They were Ojibways,' Nick said. 'And they were very nice.'

'But what were they like to be with?'

'It's hard to say,' Nick Adams said. Could you say she did first what no one has ever done better and mention plump brown legs, flat belly, hard little breasts, well holding arms, quick searching tongue, the flat eyes, the good taste of mouth, then uncomfortably, tightly, sweetly, moistly, lovely, tightly, achingly, fully, finally, unendingly, never-endingly, never-to-endingly, suddenly ended, the great bird flown like an owl in the twilight, only in daylight in the woods and hemlock needles stuck against your belly. So that when you go in a place where Indians have lived you smell them gone and all the empty pain killer bottles and the flies that buzz do not kill the sweetgrass smell, the smoke smell and that other like a fresh cased marten skin. Nor any jokes about them nor old squaws take that away. Nor the sick sweet smell they get to have. Nor what they did finally. It wasn't how they ended. They all ended the same. Long time ago good. Now no good.

And about the other. When you have shot one bird flying you have shot all birds flying. They are all different and they fly in different ways but the sensation is the same and the last one is as good as the first. He could thank his father for that.

'You might not like them,' Nick said to the boy. 'But I think you would.'

'And my grandfather lived with them too when he was a boy, didn't he?'

'Yes. When I asked him what they were like he said that he had many friends among them.'

'Will I ever live with them?'

'I don't know,' Nick said. 'That's up to you.'

'How old will I be when I get a shotgun and can hunt by myself?'

'Twelve years old if I see you are careful.'

'I wish I was twelve now.'

'You will be, soon enough.'

'What was my grandfather like? I can't remember him

except that he gave me an air rifle and an American flag when I came over from France that time. What was he like?'

'He's hard to describe. He was a great hunter and fisherman and he had wonderful eyes.'

'Was he greater than you?'

'He was a much better shot and his father was a great wing shot too.'

'I'll bet he wasn't better than you.'

'Oh, yes he was. He shot very quickly and beautifully. I'd rather see him shoot than any man I ever knew. He was always very disappointed in the way I shot.'

'Why do we never go to pray at the tomb of my grandfather?'

'We live in a different part of the country. It's a long way from here.'

'In France that wouldn't make any difference. In France we'd go. I think I ought to go to pray at the tomb of my grandfather.'

'Some time we'll go.'

'I hope we won't live somewhere so that I can never go to pray at your tomb when you are dead.'

'We'll have to arrange it.'

'Don't you think we might all be buried at a convenient place? We could all be buried in France. That would be fine.'

'I don't want to be buried in France,' Nick said.

'Well, then, we'll have to get some convenient place in America. Couldn't we all be buried out at the ranch?'

'That's an idea.'

'Then I could stop and pray at the tomb of my grandfather on the way to the ranch.'

'You're awfully practical.'

'Well, I don't feel good never to have even visited the tomb of my grandfather.'

'We'll have to go,' Nick said. 'I can see we'll have to go.'